"I'm Not Sleeping With You Tonight, Tony."

"Wrong," he said pointing a finger at her. "*I'm* not sleeping with *you,* but I'm your husband whether you like it or not."

"What does that mean?" she asked.

"It means that I don't plan to tiptoe around you anymore, Rena."

He left her on the terrace and strode over to the wet bar, pouring himself three fingers of Scotch. He hated that Rena had it right this time. He *had* married her out of obligation and a sense of duty. But he hadn't expected her resentment to irk him so much.

Hell, he'd never had to beg a woman for sex in his life. And he wasn't about to start now.

Dear Reader,

Who doesn't find a champion sexy? And former race car driver Tony Carlino is that and a whole lot more. He's the man Rena Fairfield Montgomery hates with every breath she takes, but he's also the man she'd once loved. When Tony comes home to Napa to meet the terms of his father's will and run Carlino Wines, a deathbed vow to his best friend brings Tony back into Rena's life. She's a challenge he means to win, no matter the cost.

Set against the backdrop of Napa Valley where the air is flavored with the sweet pungent scent of ripening grapes and earth deep and rich with hearty vines, the first story in my NAPA VALLEY VOWS trilogy is about forgiveness and second chances and two young hearts who find their way back to each other years later with a vow that cannot be broken.

So sit back, get comfortable and have a fine glass of hearty California merlot.

Let's toast to loves lost and found again in Napa Valley!

Charlene

CHARLENE SANDS

MILLION-DOLLAR MARRIAGE MERGER

Silhouette® Desire

Published by Silhouette Books
America's Publisher of Contemporary Romance

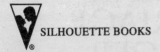

SILHOUETTE BOOKS

ISBN-13: 978-0-373-73029-2

MILLION-DOLLAR MARRIAGE MERGER

Recycling programs for this product may not exist in your area.

Books by Charlene Sands

CHARLENE SANDS

resides in Southern California with her husband, high school sweetheart and best friend, Don. Proudly they boast that their children, Jason and Nikki, have earned their college degrees. The "empty nesters" now enjoy spending time together on Pacific beaches, playing tennis and going to movies, when they are not busy at work, of course!

A proud member of Romance Writers of America, Charlene has written more than 25 romance novels and is the recipient of the 2006 National Readers' Choice Award, the 2007 Cataromance Reviewer's Choice Award and the Booksellers Best Award in 2008 and 2009. Recently *RT Book Reviews* has nominated her book, *Do Not Disturb Until Christmas* for the Best Silhouette Desire award of 2008.

To my husband, Don,
the man I've been sharing chardonnay with
for all our years. A really good man,
like a fine wine, only gets better with age.

One

From the time Tony Carlino was six years old, he'd been infatuated with cars, speed and danger. Back then, the hills of Napa that create award-winning merlot and pinot had been his playing field. Racing his dinged up scooter down the embankment, he'd hit the dirt falling headfirst into a patch of fescue grass a hundred times over. But Tony never gave up when he wanted something. He hadn't been satisfied until he'd mastered that hill with his scooter, his bicycle and finally his motorcycle. He'd graduated to stock car racing and had become a champion.

Newly retired from racing, his present fascination had nothing to do with cars and speed and everything to do with a different kind of danger.

Rena Fairfield Montgomery.

He glimpsed the blue-eyed widow from across the gravesite where dozens were gathered. Valley winds blew strands of raven hair from her face, revealing her heartbroken expression and ruffling her solemn black dress.

She hated him.

With good reason.

Soon he'd walk into a land mine of emotion and nothing posed more danger to Tony than that. Especially when it came to Rena and all she represented.

Tony glanced beyond the gravesite to those hills and Carlino land, an abundance of crimson hues reflecting off foil covering the vines, keeping grape-eating birds from destroying the crop. The land he once resented, the vines that had fed his family for generations was his responsibility now. His father had passed on just months ago, leaving the Carlino brothers in charge of the huge empire.

Once again, Tony glanced at Rena and a face devoid of emotion, her tears spent. She walked up to the bronze coffin, staring blankly, as if to say she couldn't believe this. She couldn't believe that her beloved husband, David, was gone.

Tony winced. He held back tears of his own. David had been his best friend since those scooter days. He'd been there for Tony through thick and thin. They'd kept their friendship ongoing, despite a bitter family rivalry.

Despite the fact that Rena had loved Tony first.

Rena held back a sob and bravely reached out to the blanket of fresh flowers draped along the coffin. She pulled her hand back just as her fingertip touched a rose petal. At that moment, she glanced at Tony, her sad eyes so round and blue that a piece of him unraveled.

He knew her secret.

But Tony didn't give that away. He stared at her, and for that one small moment, sympathy and the pain of losing David temporarily bonded them.

She blinked then turned around, stepping away from the gravesite, her legs weak as all eyes watched the beautiful grieving widow say her final farewell to her husband.

Nick and Joe, Tony's younger brothers, stood by his side. Joe draped an arm around him. "We're all going to miss him."

"He was as good as they come," Nick added.

Tony nodded and stared at the car as Rena drove away from the cemetery.

"Rena's all alone now," Joe said, once Nick bid them farewell. "It'll be even more of a struggle for her to keep Purple Fields going."

Tony drew a deep breath, contemplating his next move. They'd been rivals in business for years, but her winery had been failing and was barely holding on. "She won't have to."

Joe stiffened. "Why, are you planning on buying her out? She won't sell, bro. You know she's stubborn. She's had offers before."

"Not like this one, Joe."

Joe turned his head to look him in the eye. "What, you're making her an offer she can't refuse?"

"Something like that. I'm going to marry her."

* * *

Rena got into her car alone, refusing her friends' and neighbors' well-meaning gestures to drive her home, to sit with her, to memorialize David Montgomery. She never understood why people gathered after a funeral, had food catered in and specialty wines flowing. They filled their plates, chattered and laughed and most times forgot the real reason they had come. She couldn't do that to David. No, he was too young to die. Too vital. He'd been a good man, an excellent and loving husband. She couldn't celebrate his life; he'd had so much more to live. So she spoke the words with sincerity to the guests at the funeral site, "I hope you understand that I need to be alone right now," and had driven off.

She rode the lanes and narrow streets of the valley as numbness settled over her. She knew this land so well, had traveled every road, had grown up in Napa and had married here.

She wept silently. Tears that she thought were all dried up spilled down her cheeks. She found herself slowing her old Camry as she passed the Carlino estate, the vibrant vineyards sweeping across acres and acres.

She knew why she'd come here. Why she parked the car just outside the estate gates. She blamed Tony Carlino for David's death. She wanted to scream it from the hilltops and shout out the unfairness of it all.

A flashy silver sports car pulled up behind her, and she knew she'd made a mistake coming here. From the rearview mirror, she watched him step out of the car, his long legs making quick strides to the driver's side of her car.

"Oh, no." She grasped the steering wheel and rested her forehead there. Biting her lip, she took back her wish to scream out injustices. She didn't have the energy. Not here. Not now.

"Rena?"

The deep rich timbre of Tony's voice came through the window of the car. He'd been her friend once. He'd been her world after that. But now all she saw was a drop-dead handsome stranger who should have never come back to the valley. "I'm fine, Tony," she said, lifting her head from the steering wheel.

"You're not fine."

"I just buried my husband." She peered straight ahead, refusing to look at him.

Tony opened the car door, and she glimpsed his hand reaching out to her. "Talk to me."

"No…I can't," she said with a shake of her head.

"Then let's take a walk."

When she continued to stare at his hand, he added, "You came here for a reason."

She closed her eyes holding back everything in her heart, but her mind wouldn't let go of how David died. Spurred by renewed anger, she ignored Tony's outstretched hand and bounded out of the car. She strode past him and walked along the narrow road lush with greenery. From atop the hill, the valley spread out before her, abundant with vines and homes, both big and small, a hollow of land where many families worked side by side to ensure a healthy crop.

She had promised David she'd hold on to Purple Fields, an odd request from his deathbed, yet one she couldn't refuse. She loved Purple Fields. It had been her parent's legacy, and now it was her home, her sanity and her refuge.

She marched purposely ahead of Tony, which was an accomplishment in itself, since he'd always been quick on his feet. His footsteps slowed. Then he let go an exasperated sigh. "Damn it, Rena. David was my friend. I loved him, too."

Rena halted. Jamming her eyes closed momentarily, she whirled around. "You *loved* him? How can you say that? He's gone because of you!" Rena's anger flowed like the rush of a river. "You should never have come home. David was happy until you showed up."

Lips pursed, Tony jutted his jaw out. Oh, how she remembered that stubborn look. "I'm not responsible for his death, Rena."

"He wouldn't have gotten behind the wheel of that race car if you hadn't come home. When you showed up, that's all David talked about. Don't you see? You represented everything David wanted. You ran away from the vineyards. You raced. You won. You became a champion."

Tony shook his head. "It was a freakish accident. That's all, Rena."

"Your return here brought it all back to him," she said solemnly.

"My father died two months ago. I came home to run the company."

Rena glared at him. "Your father," she muttered. Santo Carlino had been a harsh, domineering man who'd wanted to build his empire no matter the cost. He'd tried to buy out every small winery in the area. And when the owners refused, he'd managed to ruin their business somehow. Purple Fields had seen the brunt of the Carlino wrath for years. Yet her parents had fought him tooth and nail, keeping their small patch of life out of Carlino hands. "I'll not speak ill of the dead, but…"

"I know you despised him," Tony stated.

Rena stuck to her promise and held her tongue about Santo Carlino, but she couldn't help how she felt and made no apologies for those feelings. "Go away, Tony."

Tony's lips curved up, a sinful, sexy curl of the mouth that at one time had knocked her senseless. "This is my land."

She slumped her shoulders. "Right."

Rena inhaled sharply, mentally chastising herself for driving up here—a bonehead move, as David would say. She was even more remorseful that she'd taken this short walk with Tony.

With hasty steps she brushed by him, but his reach was long and painfully tender when he caught her arm. "Let me help."

A lump formed in her throat. He didn't know what he was asking. She'd never accept his help. She glanced into dark, piercing, *patient* eyes. That was something for the record books—a patient Tony Carlino. He hadn't become a national stock car champion from his ability to wait.

She shook her head briskly. "Please don't touch me."

Tony glanced at his hand lying gently on her arm,

then stroked the length of it, sliding his hand freely up and down. "I mean it, Rena. You need me."

"No, I'll never need you." She jerked her arm free. "You just want to ease your guilty conscience."

Tony's eyes grew hard and sharp.

Good.

She didn't need his help or his pity. She'd done without him for twelve years and didn't need anything he had to offer. All she wanted was to curl up in her bed and dream about the day when she'd hold her precious baby in her arms.

Tony rubbed his aching shoulder and stretched out his legs, closing the Carlino books for the day. His racing injuries had a way of coming back to haunt him whenever he sat at his father's desk. Maybe it was because Santo never wanted him to leave Napa. He'd chosen racing over the family business and had left it all behind twelve years ago.

He'd wanted more than grapes and vines and worrying about the weather, crops and competition. Of course, Santo Carlino hadn't taken it lightly. He'd cursed and complained and refused to speak to Tony when he'd left.

Tony pursued his dream despite his father's tirades. Being the oldest of three sons Tony was expected to take over the business one day with his brothers by his side. But as it turned out none of the three sons had stayed home to run the Carlino empire.

Now with Santo gone, Tony had no choice but to return. His father's last will and testament made sure that each of his sons spent some time together running the company. He'd stipulated that in order for any of them to claim their inheritance, the land, the company, the Carlino empire, one of them had to agree to become the new CEO within six months.

It was just another way for his father to manipulate them. But Tony hadn't come back to Napa for the money. He had plenty of his own. He'd come back to lay his father to rest and to let his weary body recover from injuries garnered in a wreck at Bristol Raceway just months before.

He'd called his younger brothers home. Joe, the real brain in the family, had been living in New York, trying to develop the latest software phenomenon. And Nick, the youngest, had been creating havoc in Europe, earning a reputation as a gambler and ladies' man.

Tony smiled at that. Little Nick had a wild streak that could lay shame to a young and virile Santo Carlino in his bachelor days. But if one thing could be said about his old man, it was that he was a loving and faithful husband. Tony's mother, Josephina, had tempered him with love and adoration. Many thought her a saint for putting up with Santo, but only the family knew that Santo would have died for her.

"So when's the wedding?" Joe entered the office at Carlino Wines with his hands on his hips, his studious dark brown eyes visible behind a pair of glasses.

When Tony glanced at him in question, Joe continued, "You told me you were getting married."

Tony shoved the ledger books away and leaned back in his chair. "You need a willing bride for a wedding."

"Wanna tell me why you chose Rena? Is it Purple Fields you're after? Or something else?"

A sigh emerged from deep in Tony's chest. He rubbed tension from his forehead. "Maybe I want it all."

"*Want* or need?"

Tony narrowed his eyes and gave his brother a look.

Joe shrugged in an offhanded way. "You've never spoken of marriage before. And the last thing I thought I'd hear at David's funeral was that you intended to marry his widow. Even if it is Rena. We all know she's not exactly your biggest fan."

Tony scoffed. How well he knew. "Hardly that."

"So, what is it? Do you love her?"

Tony's face crinkled up, despite his efforts to keep a blank expression. The truth was he had loved Rena when they'd been younger but he'd loved racing more. He wound up breaking her heart by leaving her behind to pursue his dreams.

Now he had a chance to make it up to her and honor the pledge he'd made David. At the time he'd made that vow it was a no-brainer. David was on his last breaths, and he'd implored Tony to take care of Rena and the child he'd suspected she carried. Tony hadn't flinched when he'd made that promise.

Did Tony want to marry Rena and raise a child that wasn't his? He simply didn't know. But it was what he planned to do.

"No, I don't love her." He stood and looked his brother straight in the eyes, lowering his voice. "This goes no further."

Joe nodded.

"I made David a promise to take care of Rena, the winery and…and their unborn child."

Joe pressed a finger to the bridge of his glasses, securing them in place. He contemplated a moment staring back at Tony then gave an understanding nod. "Got it. Rena knows nothing about this I suppose."

"Nothing."

"Are you seeing her?"

Tony winced, thinking back on the excuses she'd given him. "I've tried several times since the funeral."

"Not cooperating is she?"

"No."

"Can't imagine why she doesn't want to start up right where you left off twelve years ago," Joe said, mockingly. "She picked up the pieces after you left her. It was a hard fall, Tony. I remember hearing all about it. When she fell for David, everyone thought it was the right move. They were happy for her. Sorry, but your name was mud around here for a long time. Then you started winning races and people forgot about the pain you caused Rena. Except Rena. She never forgot. She really loved David, and now he's gone. You can't blame her for hard feelings. She's had it rough."

"I don't blame her. But I will honor my promise to David."

Joe grinned. "I respect your determination, Tony. How are you going to charm a woman who clearly…"

"Hates me?" Tony huffed out a breath. Unfortunately, what he had in mind didn't require a multitude of charm.

Just blackmail. He would give Rena what she wanted most in life. "I have a plan."

Joe shook his head. "You always do."

"It's time I set that plan in action."

Two

Rena looked in her closet as tears streamed down her face. It had been three weeks since the funeral, and David's clothes—his shirts and pants, his jackets and sweatshirts—still hung just beside hers. She reached out to touch his favorite blue plaid shirt. Her fingers lingered a bit and an image appeared of sitting by a cozy fire cuddling up next to David and laying her head on the soft flannel, his arm wrapped around her shoulder. She smiled at the memory, even through her tears. "What now, David?" she asked in the solitude of her bedroom.

She was a thirty-one-year-old widow. She never would have believed it. Not when just weeks ago she'd planned on telling David her joyous news…that they were to become parents. She'd had it all planned. She'd silk-screened T-shirts that said, "I'm the Daddy" and another that said, "I'm the Mommy" and the third tiny T-shirt said, "And I'm the Boss." She'd planned on giving David the set of them over his favorite dinner.

She hadn't gone to the doctor yet, relying solely on the pregnancy test she'd taken. She'd wanted David by her side when they heard the news officially. Now she'd be going to all of her appointments alone, facing an unknown future.

The only bright spot in all this sadness was the child she carried. She loved her baby with all of her heart and vowed to protect it, doing whatever it took to make a good life for him or her.

Rena closed the closet door unable to remove and discard David's clothes as she'd planned. "I'm not ready to let go," she whispered. She needed David's things around her, to feel his presence and warmth surround her. It gave her a sense of peace, odd as that might seem.

"Do you want me to help you with David's things, Rena?" Solena Melendez's voice broke into her thoughts. Rena turned to find her friend at the bedroom threshold, a concerned look on her face.

Rena smiled sadly. Since David's death, Solena made a point to check up on Rena every morning.

"Solena, no. But thank you." Solena and Raymond Melendez worked at Purple Fields—Solena in the wine-tasting room, Raymond overseeing the vineyards. They'd been loyal employees since Rena and David took over the winery after her parents' deaths.

"It will take time, Rena."

Rena understood that. She'd lost both of her parents. She knew the process of grieving. "I know."

"And when it's time, I will help you."

She smiled and wiped away her tears. "I appreciate that." She reached for Solena, and they embraced. Their relationship had grown over the years, and now Rena thought of Solena and Raymond as more than employees—they were dear friends. Friends whose salaries she may not be able to pay if she didn't get this bank loan.

"We have orders today," Solena said, breaking their embrace. "I'll make sure they go out on time."

"Orders are good," Rena acknowledged with a nod of her head. Thankfully, Solena reminded her daily that she had a winery to run. Purple Fields was small but well-respected, and they'd been holding their own until a slowing economy and bigger wineries started shoving them out. Smaller vintners weren't able to compete and sustain the same degree of losses as the more established ones.

"I have an appointment at the bank today." Though Rena held out little hope, she had to try. She needed a loan to make her payroll this month and next. She was due a small amount from David's life insurance policy, and that money would pay for her doctor bills and whatever was left over would go in trust for her child's future. No one knew about the child she carried as yet, and she'd planned to keep it that way for the time being. She'd not told a soul. Not even Solena.

"I will pray for good news," Solena said.

"So will I," Rena said.

Rena lingered a bit after Solena left her room, putting a little makeup on a face that had seen too many tears. With dark circles beneath her eyes, no amount of makeup could hide her despair. Her grief would be evident, yet she had enough pride to want to appear in control of her emotions when she met Mr. Zelinski at the bank. Bankers were wary of desperation. Rena understood that and prepared herself with facts and figures she hoped would prove that Purple Fields was holding its own and worth the risk of a loan.

Rena walked down the stone hallway and made it to the living room when a knock sounded at her door. "Who could that be?" she muttered, taking up her purse and the file folder for her bank appointment and tucking it under her arm.

She opened the door to Tony Carlino. More than surprised, Rena blinked. "Tony? What are you doing here?"

He cast her a grim smile. "You wouldn't return my phone calls."

"There's a reason for that. I don't care to talk to you."

"Maybe not," Tony said. "But I have to talk to you."

Rena took in a steady breath and calmed her nerves. Just the sight of Tony brought bad memories. She'd gotten over him once and had moved on with her life. She certainly didn't want anything to do with him now. "What could you possibly have to say to me?"

Tony glanced inside her home. He'd been here before many years ago, but she certainly didn't want to invite him in. She'd never minded that she'd come from humble beginnings and that her family home was cozy and rustic, where the Carlino mansion had four wings of stately elegance, two dozen rooms, Italian marble and ancestral artwork that went back a few generations.

"What I have to say can't be said on your doorstep, Rena."

Rena glanced at her watch. "I'm on my way out. I don't have time to talk to you."

"Then have dinner with me tonight."

"Dinner?" Rena had to focus hard not to wrinkle her face. "No, I won't have dinner with you."

Tony let go an exasperated sigh. "I don't remember you being so difficult."

She hadn't been when she'd first met Tony at the age of sixteen. She'd taken one look at him and had fallen in love. They'd been friends first, Rena keeping her secret that she'd fallen hard for a Carlino. Tony had a smile that lit up her heart, and when they laughed together, Rena thought she'd died and gone to heaven. It had been painful holding in her feelings, not letting on that she loved him. It didn't help matters that Santo Carlino was trying to run her parents out of business.

"You don't know me anymore, Tony." Rena lifted her chin. "If this is about easing your conscience about David, you're wasting your time."

Tony's face tightened. His dark eyes grew cold. He stared at her for a moment, then as if gathering all his patience, he took a deep breath. "I haven't got a guilty conscience, Rena. But what I have to say *is* about David."

Rena glanced at her watch again. It wouldn't do to be late for her appointment, yet he'd caught her curiosity. "What about David?"

"Have dinner with me and I'll tell you."

Pressed for time and jittery about her bank appointment, Rena relented. "Fine, I'll have dinner with you."

"I'll pick you up at eight."

"Okay, now at the risk of being rude, I really have to leave."

With a quick nod of agreement, Tony left and Rena breathed a sigh of relief. She wouldn't think about seeing him later and breaking bread with him. She'd seen the determined look on his face and knew he wouldn't take no for an answer. Frankly, she didn't have time to argue. The bank appointment was all she could focus on. "One hurdle at a time." She mumbled David's favorite words of encouragement every time they'd faced a challenge.

She had more important things to worry about than having dinner with Tony Carlino.

Tony drove out of the Purple Fields gates and turned right driving along the roads that would lead him to the Carlino estate. Vineyards on both sides of the highway spread across the valley rising up hills and down slopes, covering the land in a blanket of green.

He'd only been home about three months, and he still felt disoriented, unsure of his place here in Napa. He'd come home because his father had been ill. And now, as the oldest son, he had to assume responsibility for the business working alongside his two brothers. His father had expected as much from him.

The timing had been right for his return. He'd made his mark on NASCAR and had enjoyed every minute of his career until a crash and injury took him off the racing circuit. Perhaps it had been an omen to quit, but it wasn't until his father's passing that Tony realized he'd had no choice but to leave the racing world behind.

Somewhat.

He still had endorsement deals with various companies, and that could be an advantage to Carlino Wines. The Carlino name meant success, and people identified with that. Yet Tony's life had changed so drastically in such a short span of time, and now he planned on taking on a new responsibility with a wife and child.

Was he ready for that?

He questioned that reality now. His vow to David never far from his mind, Tony admitted, if only to himself, that Rena had been right about one thing. If he hadn't come home and rekindled their friendship, David would still be alive today.

Tony approached the Carlino estate and pressed the remote that opened the wide iron gates. He parked the car in front of the garage house and exited. He met up with Joe in the driveway, his brother ever the optimist wearing a smile and horn-rimmed glasses, slapped him on the back. "You look like you've seen a ghost."

He had, in a way. Visions of David's tragic death played in his head ever since he'd driven away from Purple Fields.

It had been a glorious afternoon in Napa, the temperatures in the low seventies with fresh sunshine warm in the air—a day that made you glad to be alive. Tony remembered thinking that, right before he witnessed David's crash.

Before he knew it, he was riding beside David in the ambulance.

"I think she's pregnant," David whispered, struggling to get the words out.

"Shh. Hang on, David. Please. Save your strength."

Tony's plea didn't register with David. He continued, his voice so low that Tony had to bend over to hear him.

"She won't drink," he'd confessed, and Tony immediately understood. Vintners drank wine like others drank water.

David's coherent pleas gave Tony hope, though he appeared so weak. So fragile.

"Tony," he'd implored.

"I'm here." He knew whatever David had to say must be important.

"Don't leave her alone. She deserves a good life. Promise me you'll take care of her. And our baby."

"I promise, David. I'll take care of Rena," Tony whispered, looking deep into David's fading eyes.

"Marry her," David said, grasping Tony's hand. *"Promise me that, too."*

And Tony hadn't hesitated. He squeezed David's hand. "I'll marry her."

David gave the slightest tip of a nod and closed his eyes. "Tell her I love her."

"Hang on, David. She's coming. You can tell her yourself."

Frantic, Rena rushed up to David the minute they'd reached the hospital. They'd had time together, spoke their last words and Tony hung back giving them privacy. When David let go, Rena cried out. Her deafening sobs for David shook Tony and reached deep into his soul. He'd never seen a woman fall apart like that.

Tony shifted back to the present and looked at his brother with a shake of his head. "I saw Rena today."

Joe wrinkled his nose and gave an understanding nod. "Which explains the haunted look in your eyes. Thinking of David, too?" he asked with genuine concern.

"Yeah, he's never far from my mind. I'm the race car driver. I'm the one taking risks, yet he was the one to die in a crash."

"People die every day in car accidents." Then Joe caught himself. He didn't have a cruel bone in his body. "Sorry, I didn't mean to sound callous, but you didn't encourage him to get behind the wheel. And it *was* an accident."

"I wish Rena felt that way. It would make what I have to do a whole lot easier."

"So, it didn't go well today?"

Tony shrugged. "She blew me off, but not before I made a dinner date with her."

"That's a start. It should get easier now."

Tony scratched his chin, the stubble grating his fingers. "Doubtful. Rena is as proud as she is stubborn."

"I hear you, Tony. I've learned my lesson with the opposite sex. No more relationships for me."

Tony looked his brother in the eye. "Sheila really did a number on you, didn't she?"

Joe lifted his shoulders in a nonchalant shrug. "I'm over it."

Tony believed him, noting the firm set of his jaw and his cool air of confidence, despite his casual shrug. Joe's gorgeous New York assistant had played him, using her charms to snare him into an engagement. But the minute a wealthier man had shown interest in her, she'd dumped Joe for greener pastures and married a man who was twice her age. Joe had been burned, and he wasn't going near the fire any time soon.

"I'm on my way to the downtown office," he said, changing the subject. "Good luck with Rena tonight."

"Thanks. And Joe, keep this quiet." It wouldn't do for news to get out that Tony was dating his friend's new widow.

"I've got your back, bro."

Rena parked her car outside her home, her hands frozen on the steering wheel as she looked with numbing silence at the house in desperate need of paint and a roof that had seen better days. Her garden had been neglected lately, the grounds and outer buildings weren't what they once were. But the vineyards beyond, whose budding grapes were the mainstay of her legacy, had the best terroir in the vicinity. Their merlot and cabernet wines won awards from the combination of good weather, soil and minerals. The vineyards had never let her down. "All I have left are those vines," she mumbled, her voice shaky. "What am I going to do?"

The news from Mr. Zelinski wasn't good. She hadn't known the lengths David had gone to in order to keep them in business until she'd pressed the banker to be brutally honest. She saw regret in his eyes and sympathy cross his features and knew of his reluctance to tell her the ultimate truth. Both the Fairfield and Montgomery families were part of the tightly knit Napa community and had been personal friends of the banker. She assumed it was out of respect for her mourning that he hadn't been knocking at her door demanding his money.

The grim news she received shook what little hope she had left. Not only couldn't she qualify for a loan but David had taken out a home equity line of credit to keep them going these past few months. Until that loan was repaid and her credit restored, she couldn't even think about asking for additional help from the bank.

She owed more money than she originally thought.

Tears welled in her eyes as the hopelessness of her situation enveloped her. From across the driveway, out among the vines she spotted Raymond checking the leaves, making sure the grapes were healthy.

A sob escaped. She knew what she had to do, and it hurt to even think it. She couldn't pay Solena and Raymond. She'd barely scraped up enough money to give them their last month's salary. She'd let her other employees go, but hoped she could keep her friends on. Now, it was clear she had to let them go as well.

Her heart breaking, Rena bounded out of the car and ran up the steps to her house, tears spilling down her cheeks. She couldn't face losing them, not after losing David so abruptly. Everything around her was changing too fast.

Yet she couldn't expect Solena and Raymond to stay. She knew they'd have no trouble finding employment at another vineyard. Both were efficient, dedicated and knew as much about winemaking as she did. Selfishly, she wanted to keep them close, to have them work the land and be here when she needed them. Rena had sad facts to face, and she didn't know if she was up to the challenge.

Slamming the door shut, she strode to her bedroom, wiping at tears that continued to fall. She tossed her files and purse aside, kicking off her shoes as she flopped down on her bed. She lay looking up at the ceiling, searching her mind for a way to keep her business afloat. What avenues had she missed? Who could she turn to for help? Finally, after a half hour of torturous thought, she came up with the only solution that made sense. She had no other option.

She had to sell Purple Fields.

Three

Tony debated whether to bring Rena flowers, remembering that she'd always loved the tulips that grew in the Carlino garden. "I like the purple ones best," she'd said when they were teens. "They're bright and happy, just waiting to put a smile on someone's face."

But he knew giving Rena her favorite flowers wouldn't put a smile on her face now. Nothing he could do—aside from vanishing off the face of the earth—would do that. He'd opted to knock on her door empty-handed, hoping that she hadn't changed her mind about tonight.

He'd sort of bulldozed her into this dinner date. What other choice did he have? He'd waited a respectable amount of time to approach her, allowing her time to heal from the shock of losing her husband. Yet, with a baby on the way and a failing business, Rena was in trouble. Tony didn't think he could wait much longer.

He'd promised David.

He drove his Porsche through the Purple Fields gates for the second time today and parked in front of the gifts shop-wine-tasting room adjacent to the main house. The quaint shop attracted tourists during the late spring and summer months when the weather was mild and the scent of grapes flavored the air. Rena had worked there during high school, serving sandwiches and cheese and crackers to their customers.

Tony ran a hand down his face, bracing himself for Rena's wrath. She wouldn't agree to his terms lightly, if at all. He got out of the car and walked the distance to the house. Using the metal knocker on the door, he gave three firm raps and waited. When she didn't come, he knocked again, louder.

"Rena," he called out.

He gazed over the grounds as the last remnants of evening light faded. Focusing intently, he glanced around at the other buildings and through the vineyards. There was no sign of her. Tony tried the doorknob, and to his surprise it opened.

She'd left the door unlocked.

He felt a surging sense of alarm. Rena lived alone now. It wasn't like her not to be cautious. Without hesitation, he walked inside the house. The entry that led to the living room was dark. As he took a few steps inside, it seemed the entire house was dark. "Rena?"

He made his way down the long hall and opened one door, peering inside to an empty room. He checked another room without success. When he got to the end of the hallway, he found the last door open. A small amount of moonlight illuminated the middle of the room where Rena slept on her bed.

Tony winced, seeing her sleeping soundly, her chest lifting and falling peacefully, her raven hair spread across the pillow. A few strands curled around her face and contrasted against her creamy complexion. She wore the same austere dress he'd seen her in earlier today, but it couldn't conceal the feminine slope of her breasts or the luscious curve of her hips.

Tony had loved her once. He'd taken her virginity when she was eighteen. When she'd cried, overwhelmed by emotion, he'd clung to her and assured her of his love. Rena had given herself to him one hundred percent and though he'd tried to give her everything she needed from him, he couldn't. He had another great passion—racing. It was in his blood. From the time he was a small boy, Tony needed to feel the wind at his back. He loved speed and thrilled at the danger of being wild and free. Later, he'd learned to harness his passion. He'd learned that precision and accuracy as well as spirit made you a winner.

He'd achieved his goals without much struggle. He'd been born to race. But he'd also disappointed his father by not working alongside him as was expected by the eldest son, and he'd hurt the girl he'd admired and loved most in the world.

Memories flashed again, of making love to Rena and how incredibly poignant and pure it'd been. But Tony's mission here wasn't to rehash the past but to move on to the future. Rena was David's widow now, and the strain of his death was evident on her beautiful face, even in sleep.

His first inclination was to quietly leave, locking the door behind him, but he found he couldn't move, couldn't lift his eyes away from her sad desolate face. So he stood at the threshold of her bedroom, watching her.

It wasn't long before she stirred, her movements lazy as she stretched out on the bed. Tony's gaze moved to the point where her dress hiked up, exposing long beautiful legs and the hint of exquisite thighs.

His body quickened, and he ground his teeth fighting off lusty sexual thoughts. Yet, quick snippets of memory emerged of hot delicious nights making love to her all those years ago.

Rena opened her eyes and gasped when she spotted his figure in the doorway. Immediate fear and vulnerability entered her eyes. She sat straight up, and when she recognized him, anger replaced her fear. "What are you doing here?"

"We had a date."

"A date?" To her credit, she did appear hazily confused. Then the anger resurfaced. "How'd you get in?"

"The door was unlocked. Not a good habit, Rena. Anyone could have gotten into your house."

"Anyone *did*."

Tony chose to ignore the swipe.

Rena swung her legs around and set her bare feet on the floor. She rubbed her forehead with both hands and shook her head. "I guess I fell asleep. What time is it?"

"Eight-fifteen."

She looked up at him. "Were you standing there all that time?"

"No," he lied. "I just got here. I was fashionably late."

She closed her eyes briefly. "I don't know what happened. I felt exhausted and fell into a deep sleep."

The baby, Tony thought. He'd had many a racing buddy speak about their wife's exhaustion during their early pregnancy. "Maybe it's all catching up with you. You've been through a lot this past month."

"You don't know what I've been through." She was being deliberately argumentative, and Tony didn't take the bait.

"How long before you can be ready?"

Her brows furrowed. "Ready?"

"For dinner."

"Oh, I don't think so. Not tonight. I'm not—" she began to put her hand to her flat stomach, then caught herself "—feeling well."

"You'll feel better once you eat. How long since you've eaten?"

"I don't know…. I had a salad for lunch around noon."

"You need to keep up your strength, Rena."

She opened her mouth to respond, then clamped it shut.

"I'll wait for you in the living room."

Tony turned and walked away, not really giving her

a choice in the matter. There were many more things he'd have to force upon her before the evening was through.

Rena got up from her bed, moving slowly as she replayed the events of the day in her mind. First, Tony had visited her this afternoon, a fact that still irked her. Yet he had something to say and he wouldn't leave until he got it off his chest. That's how Carlinos operated; they did what they darn well wanted, no matter how it affected other people. Bitter memories surfaced of her father standing up to Santo Carlino, but Rena shoved them out of her mind for the moment. She couldn't go there now.

Next came thoughts of her conversation with Mr. Zelinski at the bank. He'd been kind to her, confessing his hands were tied. She wouldn't be getting the loan she desperately needed. She wouldn't be able to pay her employees. Purple Fields was doomed.

Her head began to pound. She felt faint. Though her appetite had been destroyed today, she admitted that she really should eat something. For the baby's sake, if nothing else. She couldn't afford to sink into depression. It wouldn't be good for the unborn child she carried.

As quick as her body allowed, she got ready, cringing at her reflection in the mirror. Her face was drawn, her hair wild, her clothes rumpled. She washed her face, applied a light tint of blush to her cheeks, some lipstick to her lips and brushed her hair back into a clip at the base of her neck—just to appear human again. She changed her clothes, throwing on a black pair of pants and a soft knit beige sweater that ruffled into a vee and looked stylish though comfortable. She slipped her feet into dark shoes and walked out of the room. Whatever Tony had in mind, she certainly wasn't going to dress up for him.

Tony closed the magazine he was reading and rose from the sofa when she strode in. She squirmed under his direct scrutiny. "You look better."

She didn't comment yet noted genuine concern in his eyes. Why?

He strode to the door and opened it. "Shall we go?"

"Where are you taking me?"

Tony's expression flattened. He'd caught her meaning. "I've made arrangements, Rena. No one will see you with me."

If she weren't so upset about *everything,* her face might have flamed from his acknowledgment. She lifted her chin. "How's that possible?"

"We own half of Alberto's. It's closed to the public tonight."

"You mean you had it closed for my benefit?"

"You haven't had any use for me since I returned. I didn't think you'd like answering questions about being out with me tonight if anyone saw us."

Rena had almost forgotten that the Carlinos had their hands in other enterprises. They owned a few restaurants as well as the winery. They also owned stores in outlying areas that sold a line of products related to wine.

"This isn't a date, Tony. Just so we're clear."

Tony nodded. "Very clear."

Rena strode past him and waited for him to exit her house before she locked the front door. She moved quickly, and once he beeped his car alarm, she didn't wait for him to open the car door. She climbed into his Porsche and adjusted the seat belt.

"Ready?" he asked unnecessarily. Once they made eye contact, he roared the engine to life. "It's a nice night. Mind if I put the top down?"

"No, I could use a good dose of fresh air."

It's how Tony liked to drive, with the top down, the air hitting his face, mastering the car and the road beneath.

He hit a button, and mechanically the car transformed. He drove the road to Napa surprisingly slowly, as if they were out for a Sunday drive. Every so often, he glanced her way. She couldn't deny his courtesy.

Or the fact that she thought him the most devastatingly handsome man she'd ever met. She'd thought so since they'd first met the day he entered public school at the age of sixteen. Up until that point, the Carlinos had gone to an elite private school. But Tony hated the regimented lifestyle, the solitude and discipline of being in an academy. Finally, his father had relented, granting his sons the right to go through the public school system.

Tony had made a lasting impression on her, and they'd started out as friends. But the friendship had grown as they'd gotten closer, and Rena had become Tony's steady girlfriend two years later.

Despite his obvious wealth and place in Napa society.

Despite the fact that Santo Carlino and her father had become bitter enemies.

Despite the fact that Rena never *truly* believed she could have a lasting relationship with Tony.

"Care for some music?" he asked, reaching for the CD player button.

"If you don't mind, I'd like to be quiet."

She didn't want to rekindle memories of driving in Tony's car with the top down and the music blasting. Of laughing and telling silly jokes, enjoying each other's company.

"Okay," he said amiably.

They drove in silence, Tony respecting her wishes. Shortly, he pulled into Alberto's back parking lot. "I usually don't resort to back alley entrance ways," he said, with no hint of irritation. "Are you hungry?"

"Yes, actually quite hungry."

"Good, the food is waiting for us."

Before she managed to undo her seat belt, Tony was there, opening the car door for her. He reached his hand inside, and rather than appearing incredibly stubborn in his eyes, she slid her hand in his while he helped her out. The Porsche sat so low to the ground she would have fumbled like an idiot anyway, trying to come up smoothly to a standing position.

Sensations ripped through her instantly. The contact, the intimate way his large hand enveloped her smaller one, trampled any false feeling of ease she'd imagined. She fought the urge to whip her hand away. Instead, she came out of the car and stood fully erect before slipping her hand out of his. Composing herself, she thanked him quietly and followed him inside the restaurant.

"This way," he said and gestured to a corner booth lit by candlelight. True to his word, the entire restaurant was empty but for them. She sat down at one end of the circular booth, while he sat at the other.

The few times Rena had come here, she'd always felt as though she'd wandered in from the streets in Tuscany with its old world furnishings and stone fountains. Alberto's was one of finest restaurants in the county, serving gourmet fare and the best wines from Napa.

"I had the chef prepare a variety of food. I wasn't sure what you liked."

"You forgot that I loved pepperoni pizza?"

Tony's mouth twisted. "No one could inhale pizza like you, Rena. But I doubt it's on the menu tonight. Let's go into the kitchen and see what the chef conjured up for us."

Tony bounded up from the booth and waited. She rose and walked beside him until they reached the state-of-the-art kitchen. They found covered dishes on the immaculate steel counter along with fresh breads, salads and a variety of desserts sitting in the glass re-frigerator.

Tony lifted one cover and announced. "Veal scaloppine, still hot."

Rena looked on with interest.

Tony lifted another cover. "Linguine arrabiatta, black tiger shrimps with bacon and garlic."

Steam rose up, and she leaned in closer. "Hmm, smells good."

He lifted two more covers displaying filetto di bue, an oven roasted filet mignon, which smelled heavenly but was too heavy for Rena's tastes, and ravioli di zucca, which Tony explained was spinach ravioli with butternut and Amaretto filling. Since entering the aromatic kitchen, Rena's appetite had returned wholeheartedly.

"The ravioli looks good," she said. "And that salad." She pointed to a salad with baby greens, avocado, tangerines and candied walnuts.

"Great," Tony said lifting the covered dish of her choice. And one for him. "If you could grab that salad, we'll eat. Soon as I find us a bottle of wine."

"Oh, no wine for me," she announced. Tony glanced at her with a raised brow but didn't question her. "I'll have water."

"Your poison," he said with a smile. He set the dishes down on the table and took off again, bringing back a bottle of Carlino Cabernet and a pitcher of water.

They settled in for the meal in silence, Rena polishing off the delicious salad within minutes and Tony sipping his wine, eyeing her every move. "Quit looking at me."

"You're the best looking thing in this place."

She squeezed her eyes shut. "Don't, Tony."

He shrugged it off. "Just stating the obvious."

When he turned on the charm, he had enough for the entire Napa Valley and then some. "Do you mind telling me what's so important that you couldn't tell me earlier this afternoon?"

"After dinner, Rena."

With her water glass to her lips, she asked, "Why?"

"I want you to eat your meal."

She gathered her brows and shook her head. "Because...what you have to say might destroy my appetite?"

Tony inhaled sharply then blew out the breath. "Because you're hungry and exhausted, that's why."

"Why the sudden concern about my well-being?"

Tony softened his tone. "I've always cared about you, Rena."

"No, Tony. We're not going there. *Ever,*" she emphasized. She wouldn't go down that mental path. She and Tony had way too much history, and she thought she'd never heal from the wounds he'd inflicted.

"Can't you just forget for a few minutes who I am and who you are? Can't we break bread together quietly and enjoy a good meal?"

Rena relented but still questioned Tony's mysterious behavior. "Fine. I'll eat before the ravioli gets cold."

"That's a girl."

She shot him a look.

He raised his hands up in surrender. "Sorry." Then he dug into his filet mignon with gusto and sipped wine until he'd drained two goblets.

After finishing their entrées, Tony cleared the dishes himself, refusing Rena's help. He needed time to collect his thoughts and figure out how he was going to propose marriage to his best friend's new widow and not come off sounding callous and cruel. There was only one route to take and that was to tell her the truth.

Hell, he hadn't ever really thought about marriage to anyone *but* Rena Fairfield. As teenagers, they'd spent many a night daydreaming of the time when they'd marry. But then Rena's mother became ill, and Tony had been given a real opportunity to pursue his dream of racing stock cars. Leaving Rena behind to care for her ailing mother and help her father run Purple Fields had been the only black spot in an otherwise shining accomplishment. Begging her to join him served no purpose. She couldn't leave. She had family obligations. She loved making wine. She loved Purple Fields. She was born to live in Napa, where Tony had been born to race.

He'd hurt her. No, he'd nearly destroyed her.

Each time he'd called her from the racing circuit, she'd become more and more distant. Until one day, she asked him not to call anymore. Two years later, she'd married David. He hadn't been invited to the wedding.

Tony covered a tray with tiramisu, spumoni ice cream and chocolate-coated cannolis. He returned to Rena and answered her skepticism as she watched him place the food on the table. "What? Regardless of what you think, I wasn't born with a silver spoon. We had to do chores at the house. My father was a stickler for pulling your own weight."

"I would think you're one who is used to being served."

"I am. I won't deny it. Life is good now. I'm wealthy and can afford—"

"Shutting down a restaurant for the night to have a private dinner?"

"Yeah, among other things."

"I guess I should feel honored that you served me dinner. You must have a good reason."

"I do." He glanced at the desserts on the table and moved a dish of spumoni her way. "You love ice cream. Dig in."

Rena didn't hesitate. She picked up a spoon and dove into the creamy Italian fare.

Tony dipped into it as well, butting spoons with her. They made eye contact, and Rena turned away quickly. How often had they shared ice cream in the past?

After three spoonfuls of spumoni, Rena pushed the dish away. "Okay, Tony. I've had dinner with you. No one is around. So are you going to tell me why you needed to speak to me?"

"I know you hate me, Rena."

She steered her gaze toward the fountain in the middle of the dining area. "Hate is a strong word."

"So, you don't hate me?" he asked, with a measure of hope.

She looked into his eyes again. "I didn't say that."

Tony didn't flinch. He'd prepared himself for this. "What did David say to you before he died?"

She straightened in her seat, her agitated body language not to be missed. "That's none of your business."

"Fair enough. But I need to tell you what he asked

of me, Rena. I need you to hear his last words to me as I rode beside him in the ambulance."

Tears welled in her eyes. Tony was a sucker for Rena's tears. He never could stand to see her cry.

For a moment, fear entered her eyes as if hearing David's words would cause her too much pain. But then, courageously, she nodded, opening her eyes wide. "Okay. Yes, I do want to hear what he said."

Tony spoke quietly, keeping his voice from cracking. "He told me he loved you." Rena inhaled a quick breath, and those tears threatened again. "And that you deserved a good life."

"He was the kindest man," she whispered.

"His last thoughts were only of you."

A single tear fell from her eyes. "Thank you, Tony. I needed to hear that."

"I'm not through, Rena. There's more."

She sat back in her seat and leaned heavily against the back of the booth, bracing herself. "Okay."

"He asked me to to watch out for you. Protect you. And I intend to do just that. Rena, I intend to marry you."

Four

Tony might as well have said he was going to fly to the moon on a broomstick; his declaration was just as ridiculous. Still, Rena couldn't contain her shock. Her mouth dropped open. She couldn't find the words.

Her heart broke thinking that David's very last thoughts and concerns hadn't been for himself but for her. But at the same time, if what Tony had said was true, then a wave of anger built at her departed husband as well. How could he even suggest such a thing? Asking Tony to take care of her? To protect her? He was the last man on earth she trusted, and David knew that.

Didn't he?

"You can't be serious," she finally got out once a tumultuous array of emotions swept through her system.

"I'm dead serious, Rena." He pinned her with a sharp unrelenting look.

"It's ridiculous."

"Maybe. But it's David's last wishes."

"You're saying he asked you to marry me?" Rena kept a tight reign on her rising blood pressure.

Tony nodded. "I promised him, Rena."

"No, no, no, no, no, no." She shook her head so hard that her hair slipped out of its clip.

Tony held steady peering into her eyes. "Tell me what he said to you. His last words."

"He said," she began, her voice shaky, her expression crestfallen. "He said he loved me. And that he wanted me to keep Purple Fields." She looked down for a moment to compose herself. "He knew how much it meant to me."

"And you promised him?"

"I did. But I—" Flashes of her conversation with Mr. Zelinski earlier today came flooding back. There was no hope of saving the winery. As much as it hurt her, she'd resolved that she had no other option but to sell Purple Fields. Not only would her family's legacy be lost but so would her livelihood. Yet she needed to provide for her baby. That's all that mattered now, and selling out meant that she'd have enough cash for a year or two if she were very careful. "I can't keep it. I've already decided...to sell."

Tony sat back in his seat, watching as Rena tried to compose herself. So many thoughts entered her mind all at once that her head began to ache. She put her head down and rubbed her temples, to alleviate the pain and to avoid Tony's scrutiny.

"You don't want to sell Purple Fields," he said softly.

"No, of course not."

"You know what it would mean to Purple Fields if we marry? You'd have no more worry…I'd make sure of it."

She kept her head down. She didn't want to admit that marrying Tony would solve her immediate problems and she'd be able to keep her promise to David. But she also knew that her emotions would rule it out this time. She couldn't marry Tony Carlino.

He'd abandoned her when she'd needed him most.

He'd hurt her so deeply that it took a decent man like David to heal her and make her trust again. She had no faith in Tony, and marriage to anyone, much less him, was out of the question. Her wounds were still too raw and fresh.

Tony reached over and caressed her hand with his. Again, an instant current ran between them. "Think about it, Rena. Think about the promises we both made to David."

Twenty minutes later, as Tony drove her home, she still couldn't think of anything else. She wanted to save Purple Fields, to see it thrive and be successful again, but the cost was too great.

Tony walked her to the door. She slipped the key into the lock and turned to face him. "Good night, Tony."

Tony's dark eyes gleamed for a moment. He glanced at

her mouth, his gaze lingering there. Her heart pounded, and for an instant, she was that young smitten girl who banked on his every word. He leaned his body closer, his eyes on hers, and she remembered the chemistry between them, the joy of loving him and having him love her. Images that she'd thought had been destroyed came back in a flash. He slanted his head and she waited. But his kiss bypassed her lips and brushed her cheek. He grabbed the doorknob and shoved open her door. "I'll come by to see you tomorrow, Rena."

Rena stepped inside and leaned heavily on her door, her fingers tracing the cheek he'd just kissed. She squeezed her eyes shut and prayed for a way out of her dilemma.

A way that didn't include marrying Tony Carlino.

The next day, Tony knocked on Rena's door at noon. When she didn't answer the knock, he walked toward the gift shop and peeked inside the window. Solena Melendez waved to him, and he walked inside the store. "Good afternoon."

"Hello, Solena." Tony had met her at David's funeral for the first time. He'd learned enough to know that Solena and Rena were good friends, Solena being just a few years older. She lived in a residential area of Napa with her husband, Raymond, and they worked for Purple Fields since Rena and David took over from her parents. A quick glance around told him that though Solena kept the quaint gift shop immaculate, the shelves were only scantily stocked with items for sale. "I'm looking for Rena. Do you know where she is?"

"I'm right here." Rena came out of the back room, her arms loaded down with a few cases of wine.

Tony had an instant inclination to lift those heavy boxes from her arms but restrained himself. Rena was a proud woman.

She set the boxes down on the front counter. "I'll help you with these bottles in a minute." She smiled warmly at Solena and turned to Tony, her face transforming from warm to cold in a flash. "Follow me," she said and walked outside the shop and down the steps.

The air was fresh and clear, the sky above as blue as Rena's eyes. She walked past her house to the vineyards, and once they were out of earshot she turned to him. "Do you plan on showing up here whenever you want?"

Tony grinned. "Are you mad because I didn't call to make an appointment?"

"No. Yes." Her brows furrowed. "I'm busy, Tony. I don't welcome drop-by company unless they are paying customers."

"You're working with a skeleton crew. And working too hard."

Rena rolled her eyes. "I've been doing this work since I learned to walk, practically. Yes, I work hard, but I don't mind. Why are you here?"

"I told you I'd come by today."

"Checking up on me?"

"If you want to look at it that way."

Rena's face twisted in disgust. "I can take care of myself. I hate that David made you promise to watch out for me."

"I know you do. But a promise is a promise."

"And you don't break your promises, do you? Except to young girls you've pledged your heart to. Then you have no problem."

Rena turned away from him, but he couldn't let her get away with that. He reached out and grabbed her wrist, turning her around to face him. "I loved you, Rena. Make no mistake about that. I've apologized for hurting you a hundred times. But I couldn't stay here then, and you know it. And you couldn't leave with me, and you know that, too. We weren't destined to be together back then."

She yanked her arm free and hoisted her pretty chin. "We're not destined to be together ever, so why don't you go away."

"I'm not going anywhere. Not until I make myself clear. I'm offering you a business proposition, not a real marriage proposal. If you let go of some of your anger and pride, you'd see that. I'm offering you a way to save Purple Fields."

She remained silent.

"How long before you have to let Solena and her husband go? How long before you'll have to close the winery? You don't want to sell. Purple Fields is a big part of you. You love what you do."

"Don't," she said, her eyes filling with moisture. "Don't, Tony."

"Don't what? Speak the truth? You know damn well marrying me is the best thing all the way around."

"David's been gone only a short time. And…and, I don't love you." She pierced him with a direct look.

"I don't love you either," he said, softly so as not to

hurt her anymore. "But, in all these years, I've never wanted to marry another woman. I've never even come close."

He put his arms around her waist and pulled her toward him. Without pause, he brushed his lips to hers softly at first. When she didn't pull away, he deepened the kiss, relishing the exquisite softness of her lips, enjoying the woman that Rena had become. Soft, lush and incredibly beautiful.

When he broke off the kiss, he gazed into Rena's stunned blue eyes. "We may not have love anymore, but we have history and friendship."

She tilted her head stubbornly. "I'm not your friend."

"David wants this for both of us."

"No!" Rena pulled away at the mention of David's name. Confusion filled her expression, and she wiped her mouth with the back of her hand, as if wiping away all that they'd once meant to each other. "I can't marry you—no matter what you promised David. I still blame you for his death and, and..."

"And what, Rena? That kiss just proved we still have something between us. You can save your winery and honor David's last wish."

"You don't understand." Then Rena's eyes reflected dawning knowledge, as if a light had been turned on inside her head. She covered her flat stomach with her hand. "Your family prides itself on bloodlines. It's instilled in your Italian heritage. Everything has to be perfect. Everything has to be pure from the wine you make to the babies you bring into this world. Well, I'm pregnant, Tony. With David's baby. You'd be raising David's child as your own."

Tony didn't flinch. He didn't turn away. He didn't move so much as a muscle in surprise. That was his mistake. Rena expected shock. She expected him to change his mind, to withdraw his marriage proposal. It irked him that she thought so little of him.

Rena backed away, gasping at his nonresponse. Her mouth dropped open, and when she spoke, her voice broke with accusation. "You know. How? *How* do you know, Tony?" She pressed him for an answer.

"I didn't know for sure, until now."

Rena narrowed her eyes. "Tell me."

Tony sighed. "It was David. He suspected it."

Rena backed away, her hands clutching at her hair. Her shoulders slumped, color drained from her face. It was as if she relived his death all over again. She looked down at a patch of shriveled grape leaves on the ground. "He knew about our baby."

"I'm sorry, Rena."

Her eyes watered. "David won't ever meet his child."

"No, but he wanted to protect him and…you. I'm capable of doing that for you, Rena."

"But I don't want to marry you," she said softly.

Tony heard the resignation in her tone. She was considering her options. "I know."

She peered into his eyes. "How would it look? I'm barely a widow—and now I'm marrying my husband's friend."

Tony made this decision to protect Rena days ago. "No one has to know. We'll keep it secret."

"Secret?" She looked at him, puzzled.

"For a time, anyway."

She closed her eyes, contemplating. She battled with the idea of marrying him. Her facial expressions reflected her thoughts as they twisted to and fro.

He pressed his point. "Your winery needs help fast," he said quietly, and then added, "but more important, your child needs a father."

"Maybe that's true." Rena's eyes flooded with tears now, her voice filled with surrender. "But I don't need you, Tony. I'll never need you again."

That was the closest she'd come to a yes.

Tony made mental plans for their wedding day.

Rena cried herself to sleep for two nights, realizing the futility in denying the inevitable. She was cornered and had nowhere to run. She'd been waging mental wars inside her head since Tony's proposal for a secret marriage. She couldn't come up with any other viable solution to her dilemma. She was so heavily in debt she doubted she'd find anyone willing to take on such a big risk.

But how could she marry Tony?

How could she allow him to be a father to David's child?

It all seemed so unfair.

Rena stepped outside her house and squinted into the morning sunlight rising just above the hills. Golden hues cast beautiful color over the valley. This was her favorite time of day. When David was alive, she'd often wake early and come outside to tend her garden and open her mind to all possibilities. David would sit on the veranda to drink coffee and watch her. They would talk endlessly about little things and his presence would lend her peace and comfort.

But since his death, Rena had sorely neglected her garden. Today, she hoped she'd find solace working the soil and nurturing the lilies and roses. She needed this time to come to grips with what she had to do.

She put on her gardening gloves and took to the soil, yanking out pesky weeds, and with each firm tug, thoughts of what David asked from her in his death plagued her mind. He hadn't given her what she needed most—time to grieve. Time to try to figure out a way to save Purple Fields on her own. Instead, he'd hidden the facts from her and shielded her from bad news. David had always been a man she could count on, but he hadn't realized the toll his dying request would take on her.

She tugged at a stubborn weed, bracing her feet and pulling with all of her might. Emotions roiled in the pit of her stomach. Feelings she'd held in for a long time finally came forth as she felt the weed break with the ground. "I'm so mad at you, David, I could spit."

The weed released, easing from the soil slowly and Rena held it in her hands, staring at the roots that had once been secured in the earth. "You died and left me with this mess."

And when she thought tears would fall again, instead simmering anger rose up with full force. She was angry, truly angry with David. She was angry with herself.

But most of all, she was angry with Tony Carlino. Her anger knew no rationality at the moment. And for the first time since David's death, Rena felt strong in that anger. She felt powerful. She refused to let guilt or fear wash away her innermost feelings. David had let her down. Tony had blackmailed her.

But she didn't have to take it without a fight. She didn't have to lose control of everything she loved, just because fate had stepped in and knocked her down. New strength born of distress and determination lifted her. She still had a say in what happened in her life. Her primary obligation was to protect her unborn child and secure his future legacy.

Rena whipped off her gloves and stood up, arching her back and straightening out as a plan formed in her mind. With new resolve, she headed back into the house. She had a call to make. She needed expert legal advice and knew that Mark Winters, David's longtime friend, would help her.

She may be down temporarily, but she wasn't out.

For the first time in a long time, Rena felt as though she had some control about her destiny.

And it felt darn good.

Tony glanced at his watch, his patience wearing thin as he sat in a booth by the window at the Cab Café. Rena was ten minutes late. Had she backed out of this meeting at the last moment?

This morning, he'd been happy to hear Rena's voice on the phone. She'd called early, just as he was leaving for work and she'd sounded adamant that he meet with her today. She wouldn't give him a hint as to what the meeting was about, but since he'd proposed to her last week, he figured she'd come to realize that marrying him was inevitable. Not one to ever look a gift horse in the mouth, he'd cleared his schedule and shown up here five minutes early.

The boisterous teenage hangout held a good deal of memories for them both, and he wondered why she'd picked this particular place. At one time the Cabernet Café was a wine-tasting room but when that failed, the owner had changed the café's focus and now it thrived as a burger-and-fries joint.

A waitress wearing an apron designed with a cluster of purple grapes approached and Tony ordered coffee to pass the time. He decided to wait until he'd finished his first cup before calling Rena to see what the delay was.

Less than five minutes later, just as he was pulling out his cell phone, Rena stepped into the café. He rose from his seat and she spotted him. He gave her a little wave, which she ignored.

As she approached, Tony noticed she had shadows under eyes that were haunted and sad, but even that couldn't mask her genuine beauty. Her hair was pulled back from her face in a ponytail and she wore jeans and a blue sweater that brought out the sparkling hue of her eyes. Her purse sat on her shoulder but she also carried a manila folder in one hand. He waited until she reached the table and sat across from him before he took his seat.

"I was just about to call you. Thought you might have changed your mind."

She glanced at him and shook her head. "No, I'm sorry I'm late. I had an appointment this morning that ran a little long."

"What kind of appointment?" he asked, wondering what was so important to keep him waiting.

She glanced out the window, hesitating, and then turned back to him. "I had my first checkup today for the baby."

Tony leaned back against the vinyl booth and stared at her. "How did it go? Is everything okay?"

Rena couldn't seem to keep her joy from showing. She granted him a smile and her voice lifted when she spoke. "Yes, the baby is healthy. I'm due in October."

"That's good news, Rena." But the news also brought home the reality of what he was about to do. He would take responsibility for a child he didn't father. He would marry a woman who didn't love him. All of it hit him hard between the eyes. This was really happening.

He'd loved David as a friend, but he also knew that if it had been any woman other than Rena, he wouldn't have agreed to David's request. He wouldn't be doing this for a stranger. Though Rena would deny it, they had a connection. Their lives had been entwined for years. Marrying her wasn't as much a hardship for him as it was for her. "What else did the doctor say?"

She breathed out quietly. "He told me to try to stay calm. Not to let stress get me down."

"That's good advice, Rena. You've had a lot to deal with lately and you should try to relax for—"

"I don't need a lecture, Tony."

Her abrupt behavior had him gritting his teeth. Pregnant women were temperamental at times, at least that's what he'd heard from his married friends, but it was more than that with Rena. His proposal to her was nothing more than sugarcoated blackmail. Hell, he hated to add to her stress. But he owed David this and he had to see it through.

She looked at him and inhaled a deep breath. "I'm sorry. This isn't easy for me. Believe me, I have the baby's well-being in mind every second of the day. That's why it's been such a tug of war."

Tony had thicker skin than to be offended, but most women wouldn't consider a proposal from him a terrible thing.

The waitress walked up to the table again. "Hi, what can I get for you?"

Rena faced her without opening the menu. "I should have the California café salad."

"One California café salad, got it. And for you sir?"

"But," Rena interrupted and the waitress turned back to her, "I'm craving a chili cheeseburger with extra pickles."

The waitress grinned. "That's our specialty. Got it. And I'll make sure you get those pickles."

"Thank you. I'll have a lemonade too."

Tony ordered the same thing, and after the waitress left, he glanced at Rena. "You're having cravings? I wondered why you wanted to meet me here."

She lifted a shoulder and shrugged. "It's been a long

time and this morning when I got up, I couldn't stop thinking about having a chili cheeseburger."

"We sure ate our share of them when we were kids. We used to close down this place, remember?"

"Yeah, I do."

And for a moment, Rena's face softened. Tony remembered what it was like being with her back then. The fun times they'd had together. They'd been so close and so much in love.

Rena stared at the manila folder she'd set down on the table and her expression changed.

"What's going on?" Tony asked, glancing at the folder. "What's in there?"

"It's something I want from you."

Surprised, Tony looked at her, arching a brow. "Okay, so why don't you tell me?"

She slid the folder toward him. "It's a prenuptial agreement." Her eyes met his directly.

Tony hid his surprise well. He didn't react, though a dozen thoughts popped into his head all at once. He decided to hear her out and not jump to conclusions.

"If I marry you, I want Purple Fields to remain in my name. I want full ownership of the winery and vineyard. I want to have the final say in every decision having to do with it. My child will own Purple Fields one day, no questions asked. Have your attorney look it over. It's legal and there shouldn't be any problem."

Tony sighed heavily. "Rena, you do see the irony in this, don't you?"

Rena searched his eyes. "How so?"

"First of all, I don't want Purple Fields. Marrying me

has nothing to do with me getting my hands on your winery. The fact is, I'm worth tens of millions, Rena. Everything I own will be yours. I'm not asking for a prenuptial agreement from you."

"If you want one, I'd sign it."

"I don't want one, damn it! I'm not entering into this marriage lightly. If we marry, it'll be for keeps. We'll have a child and we'll be a family. Do you understand what I'm saying?"

"Yes, of course. But you've made promises to me before that you've broken, and now I have no choice in the matter. I want some control. You should understand that, being a Carlino."

Tony's lips tightened. He didn't want an argument, so he chose his words carefully. "This time it's different. This time, I'm not going to break any promises I make to you."

"I'd sleep better at night if I believed you."

Tony let go a curse.

Rena continued to explain. "I'm only protecting what's mine. Can you blame me? It's all I have left and I don't want to lose it."

Angry now, Tony didn't bother reading the agreement first. "Fine. I'll sign it."

He reached into his pocket and pulled out a pen. Then he slid the papers out and gave them only a cursory glance before signing his name at the bottom.

"Don't you want your attorney to look it over?" Rena asked, her expression incredulous, watching him slide the papers back into the folder.

He shook his head. "I know you well enough to

know there's nothing in this agreement that I'd find questionable. I *trust* you."

Rena sat back against the booth, her chin bravely raised. "I won't let you make me feel guilty about this."

"I'm not trying to make you feel guilty," Tony remarked gruffly. Then when he saw Rena holding back tears, he softened his tone. "I signed the papers. You're getting what you want—at least as far as Purple Fields is concerned. I never intended on taking that away from you." Then he braced his arms on the table and leaned in. Their gazes locked. "We have to make this work, Rena. If for nothing else but that child you're carrying."

Rena closed her eyes briefly. Her silence irritated him, as if she were trying to believe and trust in him. He wasn't like his ruthless father, but would Rena ever acknowledge that? "I know," she said finally.

Tony settled back in his seat. What was done, was done. He didn't want to rehash the past. It was time to look toward the future.

And live in the present.

Tony changed the subject as soon as the food was delivered. He wanted Rena to enjoy the meal she'd craved. Lord knew she needed to build her strength. She also needed some calm in her life and wondered if he could ever provide her that.

Without Rena actually saying so, the existence of the prenuptial agreement he'd just signed was an acceptance to his proposal.

Tony resigned himself to the fact that soon he'd be a husband to a pregnant and reluctant bride.

* * *

One week later, Rena stood beside Solena, Tony beside his brother Joe as they spoke vows before a Catholic priest in a little church just outside of San Francisco. Rena's mind spun during the entire mass thinking this was some kind of a bad joke. She couldn't believe she was actually marrying Tony Carlino, the boy she'd once loved beyond reason. The boy she'd dreamed of marrying with every breath that she'd taken. Now that dream seemed more like a nightmare.

As the priest blessed their union, Rena reminded herself of the reasons she'd made this decision.

Marrying Tony meant saving her winery from ruin.

It meant that she could honor David's last wishes.

It meant that her baby would never want for anything, much less a roof over his head or a meal on his plate.

They were good solid reasons. No sacrifice was too great for her child.

Father Charles finished the ceremony. "You may kiss the bride."

She hardly felt like a bride. She wore a pale yellow dress suit. Tony had provided her with a small calla lily bouquet and had placed a simple platinum band on her finger during the service. Out of reverence to David, he hadn't given her a diamond—she'd only just last week removed her wedding ring from her finger and tucked it away safely in her jewelry case. It had been excruciatingly hard letting go.

Tony's lips brushed hers softly. He smiled when he looked into her eyes. She granted him a small smile in return.

Joe and Solena congratulated them, their mood solemn. If Father Charles noticed the austere atmosphere at the altar, he didn't mention it. In fact, he pumped Tony's hand hard and embraced Rena.

Raymond approached with a handshake to Tony and a hug for her. Nick approached her with arms open and a big smile. "Welcome to the family. I've always wanted a sister. But I'll let you in on a little secret. I had a big crush on you in high school."

Rena chuckled and flowed into his arms. "No, you didn't."

"I did. But you were my big brother's girl." They broke their embrace and Nick stepped away, turning to Tony and slapping him on the back. "He's a lucky man. Be good to her or I might steal her away."

Tony glanced at her. "I'd like to see you try."

Rena bit her lip, holding back a smile. She'd seen the Carlino boys' teasing banter, and at times she had been a part of it. If anyone could make her laugh, it was Nick. He'd always been too clever for his own good. All the Carlino boys had their own brand of charm and she'd learned early on that each in his own way was a lady-killer.

The six of them dined in an out-of-the-way restaurant on the outskirts of San Francisco, and everyone sipped champagne when Nick proposed a toast. Rena pretended to sip hers, letting the bubbly liquid touch her mouth before she set her glass down. She was among her closest friends here, and though she'd explained to Solena and Raymond her reasons for this sudden secret marriage to Tony, she hadn't confessed about the baby yet. She needed time to come to grips with all that had changed in her life.

When the dinner was over, Rena walked outside with Solena, bidding her farewell. "I hope I'm not making a mistake."

Solena took her hand and squeezed gently. "Remember, David wanted this for you." She glanced at Tony who stood beside Raymond and his brothers. "Give him a chance," she whispered. "You loved him once."

"It's different now, Solena. There's so much hurt between us."

"I know. But if you find forgiveness, your heart will open."

Rena doubted it. She didn't know if she was capable of forgiving Tony. He'd destroyed her life not once but twice. Was she supposed to forget all that? Emotions jumbled up inside her, and she fought to control them. "I can't believe I married him."

Solena reached out to hug her tight. "It will work out as it's meant to. Be patient. And remember, I am always here if you need me."

Rena faced her and gratitude filled her heart. "I know you are." She reminded herself that if she hadn't married Tony, she wouldn't be able to employ her dear friends, and that was enough consolation for now.

Tony approached and put a hand to her back. "Are you ready to leave?"

She nodded to him and bid farewell to her friend, squeezing her hand tight. "I'll see you tomorrow, Solena."

"Yes." Solena glanced at Tony. "Congratulations."

"Thank you."

Once Raymond and Solena left, Tony took Rena's hand and guided her to his car. "You're not going to your own execution, you know."

"Did I say anything?" she quipped, slipping her hand away.

"Not in words."

She shrugged. "It's all so strange."

But before Tony could respond to that, Joe and Nick walked up. Nick smiled. "You did it, you two. *Finally.*"

Joe cleared his throat. "Let's leave them alone, Nick."

"Just wishing them well," he said. "I guess we'll see you at the house later."

Tony shook his head. "I'm not going back to the house tonight."

"You're not?" Rena's nerves jumped. She hadn't discussed with him what they'd do after they married. She'd only assumed that since the marriage was secret, he'd stay at his house and she'd stay at hers.

"No." He turned to her. "I've booked a suite at the Ritz-Carlton in San Francisco."

Joe grabbed Nick's shoulder and gave a little shove. "Let's go."

"I guess I'm going," Nick said with a cocky smile. "Congrats again, Rena. Big brother."

Rena watched them both get in the car and leave. She turned to Tony, dumbfounded. "Why did you get us a room at a hotel?"

"It's our wedding night."

She closed her eyes, praying for strength. "Surely, you don't expect—"

"You're my wife now, Rena. Did you expect me to remain celibate the rest of my life?"

Five

Rena sat stonily silent in the car all the way to the hotel, her expression grim and her pretty mouth deep in a frown. She said nothing as he checked in or on the ride in the elevator to the Presidential Suite.

A private servant opened the door and showed them inside. In awe, Rena gasped when she entered the suite.

Rich furnishings, stately artwork and a Steinway grand piano filled the living room. Tony put a hand to her back and guided her inside. The servant showed them around the suite, walking them through French doors to the master bedroom with an amazing view of San Francisco Bay, the master bathroom highlighted by a sunken whirlpool bath filled with scented flower petals, a second bedroom and an elegant dining room with seating for eight.

Once back in the living room, Tony dismissed him. "We won't need your services for the rest of the evening."

"Yes, sir," he said, and once he left the suite, Tony opened the French doors to the terrace.

"It's massive," Rena said, stepping outside and taking a deep breath of air. The sun began a slow descent on the horizon. "You could fit two of my gift shops in the terrace alone." Then she turned to him. "Why did you do this?"

"You deserve it, Rena."

Before she could respond, he turned her shoulders and pointed out toward the ocean. "Look, there's Alcatraz."

Rena focused on the island that had once been a notorious prison. "The view is amazing. All of this is amazing."

Tony kept his hands on her shoulders for a few seconds, caressing her lightly. The air fresh and clear, he breathed in and caught the subtle scent of her exotic perfume. She'd put her hair up for the wedding ceremony, giving him access to her throat. He took in another breath before he felt her stiffen. He backed away, giving her space and time to adjust to the situation and pulled out a white iron patio chair. "Sit down and enjoy the fresh air."

She did and he sat facing her. "I'm not the big bad wolf, Rena. I know this is difficult for you."

"Difficult doesn't begin to describe it. I never thought

I'd see this day." Her eyes appeared strained. Her body slumped with fatigue.

"What day?" he asked.

"The day that I'd be your wife."

"I'm not the villain here. I'm trying to do right by you and David. I'm going to save your business, take care of you and raise…our child."

Rena flinched, and regret filled her eyes. "You're trying to ease your conscience and fulfill an obligation."

Tony shook his head. "You won't cut me any slack, will you?"

"I'm sorry I'm not the doting wife you'd imagined. I can't be…this is all so unfair."

"I wish to hell David was alive, too. He was my best friend, damn it." Tony rose and paced the terrace. He hadn't planned on any of this. But he was trying to make the best out of a bad situation. He'd been patient with Rena, though she still blamed him for David's death. He'd tried to please her. He'd tried being the nice guy, yet she wanted no part of it.

Okay, the gloves were coming off.

"You're exhausted. Why don't you take a bath? It's waiting for you. Then get into bed."

Rena hoisted her chin. "I'm not sleeping with you tonight, Tony."

"Wrong," he said pointing a finger at her. "*I'm* not sleeping with *you*, but I'm your husband whether you like it or not."

"What does that mean?" She asked with real fear in her voice.

Tony was too annoyed with her to care. "It means that I don't plan to tiptoe around you anymore, Rena."

He left her on the terrace and strode over to the wet bar, pouring himself three fingers of scotch. He hated that Rena had it right this time. He *had* married her out of obligation and a sense of duty to David. But he hadn't expected her resentment to irk him so much.

Hell, he'd never had to beg a woman for sex in his life. And he wasn't about to start now.

Rena had never stayed in a hotel as extravagant as this one and decided to take advantage of her surroundings. True to Tony's word, the bathtub was steaming and waiting for her. Her body craved the warmth and tranquility a nice hot soak in a tub would provide. She closed the bathroom door and lit the candles that were strategically placed around the tub, sink and dressing area. The Ritz-Carlton knew how to pamper and she wasn't going to deny herself this pleasure. She kicked off her shoes, then stripped out of her clothes folding them neatly and setting them on the marble counter. She turned on the large LCD screen on the wall, finding a music station that played soulful jazz. All lights were turned down but for the flashing abstract images on the flat screen and the candles that burned with a vanilla scent.

Naked and relishing her impending bath, Rena stuck her toe in the water. "Perfect," she hummed, sinking the rest of her body into the exquisite warmth. For the first time in days, she relaxed.

She closed her eyes and obliterated all negative

thoughts. Instead, she thought of the baby growing inside her. She wondered if it was a boy or a girl. She hoped it would have David's kindness and intelligence and maybe her blue eyes. She hoped for so many things, but mostly she hoped her child would be happy.

A smile surfaced on her face as she pictured a sandy blond-haired little boy or a raven-haired little girl. Or perhaps a boy would have her coloring and a girl would have her father's. Either way, Rena would love that child beyond belief.

The door to the bathroom opened and Tony strode in. She gasped and sunk farther down into the tub. "What are you doing in here?"

Tony unbuttoned his shirt and dropped it onto the floor. He looked her over, his gaze following the valley between her breasts. "I'm taking a shower."

Her heart rate sped. "In here?"

"This is the master bathroom, right?"

Rena narrowed in on him. "How much have you had to drink?"

He cocked her a smile and shook his head. "Not enough, honey."

His shoes were off in a flash, and when he reached for his belt, she closed her eyes. She heard him stepping out of his clothes, open the glass shower door, then close it. The shower rained to life, and steam heated the room.

Rena opened her eyes slowly. Tony was deep into his shower, soaping himself up. She took a swallow and watched, unable to tear her gaze away. At one time, Tony Carlino was everything she wanted in life. Those old feelings surfaced, and she tried to shove them away, but it was darn hard to do. Not when he was built like a Greek god, stunningly masculine and boldly beautiful. He moved with grace and confidence, comfortable in his own skin. And so she watched him lather his body, wash his hair and let the water pelt down in streams over his broad shoulders, down the curve of his spine and into the steam that hid the rest of him from view. He turned abruptly and caught her staring. His brows elevated into his forehead, and the corners of his mouth lifted ever so slightly.

Rena turned away then, afraid that if he read her expression, he'd know what she was thinking. He'd know that some feelings can't be destroyed. Some feelings just simply…stay, no matter how hard you try to abolish them. They hide under the anger and pain, waiting.

When the shower spigot turned and the water shut off, Rena tensed. She didn't know what Tony expected. His comment about not tiptoeing around her had her perplexed. The shower door opened, and Tony stepped out, naked. Rena refused to let him intimidate her. She didn't look straight at him, but she didn't look away either. Instead she focused on a point beyond his head.

After wiping down his body, he wrapped the towel around his waist and glanced at her. "You should get out. You're getting cold."

His gaze lingered on her chest. No longer covered with flower petals and bubbles, her nipples were now visible beneath the water. She covered up and nodded. "I will, as soon as you're through in here."

Tony scrubbed the stubble on his face, contemplating.

"I guess I'll shave tomorrow. You can get out now." He reached over and handed her a plush chocolate-colored towel.

She grabbed it and hoisted it to her chin. "Well?"

"I'll be sleeping in the second bedroom. Get some rest, Rena." He bent over and kissed her on the cheek then cast her a rather odd look.

"What?" she asked, curious.

"When we were together, neither one of us would have imagined our wedding night to be anything like us."

She sighed. "No, not back then."

He nodded and left the room, leaving her with poignant and erotic memories of making love to him years ago when they'd been hot and wild for each other.

Rena slept heavily, her body needing the rest. When she woke, she snuggled into the pillow recalling her dream. She'd been out in the vineyards, the grapes ripe and ready to be picked, the air flavored with their pungently sweet aroma. She turned and David was beside her, his smile wide as he looked at the vines, then at her. "We'll have a good year." But then, David's face became Tony's. Somehow, within the eerie images of her mind, it had always been Tony out in the vineyard with her.

Disoriented, she popped her eyes open and gazed out the window as the San Francisco Bay came into view. She clung to cotton one-thousand-thread-count sheets and sat up in bed, looking around the master suite of the

Ritz-Carlton Hotel. It all came back to her now. David was dead, and she'd married Tony Carlino yesterday.

"Oh, God," she whispered.

"I see you're up." Tony stepped out of the bathroom, his face covered with shaving cream, his chest bare, wearing just a pair of black slacks.

Rena blinked, trying not to stare at his tanned, broad chest or the way he casually strode into the bedroom as if they'd been married for twenty years. "Did you sleep well?"

"Like a bab— Um, very well."

"You look rested," he said, then turned around and entered the bathroom again. She craned her neck to find him stroking a razor over his face. "Breakfast is ready if you're hungry," he called out.

She was famished. She'd discovered the first trimester meant eating for two. Finally, her appetite kicked in full force and that was good for the baby. Her child needed the nourishment and so did she. She'd been so terribly strained lately, with David's death, the failure of Purple Fields and her financial situation, that she'd lost her appetite. She'd had to force herself to eat. It was so much easier when she actually *felt* like eating.

"I'll get out of here in a sec," Tony said. "Give you time to dress. I'll wait for you in the dining room."

"Okay," she found herself saying.

Rena entered the bathroom shortly after Tony finished his shave. She splashed water on her face and combed her hair. While she'd often stay in her bathrobe during her morning breakfast routine, she found that too intimate to do with Tony. She dressed in a pair of slacks and a thin knit sweater that Solena had picked out of her wardrobe when Tony had secretly asked her friend to pack a bag for their stay here at the hotel.

Rena suspected Tony hadn't mentioned their wedding night at the Ritz to her, knowing she'd refuse. But yesterday after the wedding dinner, he'd just sprung it on her, catching her off guard. Just one more reason she didn't trust him. While others might see it as a romantic gesture, Rena felt as though she'd been deceived.

She entered the dining room and found Tony relaxing at the head of the table, reading the newspaper and sipping coffee.

He stood when she entered the room. "Morning again."

She managed a small smile then glanced at the antique sideboard filled with platters of food. "Where did all this come from?"

Tony shrugged. "It's the Presidential Suite."

"And that makes food magically appear?"

He laughed. "Yeah, I guess so."

"You might be used to being treated like this, but this is…overwhelming to me."

Tony walked over to stand before her. He searched her eyes. "I don't live like this, Rena. But it's a special occasion. I thought you deserved a little pampering." He stroked her cheek, his finger sliding along her jaw line tenderly. It had been so long since she'd been touched like this. So long since she'd had any real tenderness. She was nine weeks pregnant, and though she'd tried to be strong when David died, there were times when she just needed some gentle contact.

She looked into Tony's dark beautiful eyes, then lowered her gaze to his mouth. It was all the encouragement he needed. He took her carefully in his arms and bent his head, bringing their lips together in a soft kiss.

Rena relished his lips on hers, the gentle way he held her, the warmth and comfort he lent. It wasn't a sensual kiss but one of understanding and patience.

He surprised her with his compassion, and that made her wary. She couldn't put her faith in Tony—he'd destroyed that years ago. If she'd had any other way out of her dilemma she wouldn't have married him, despite gentle kisses and kind overtures.

"Rena, don't back off," he said.

"I have to. You offered me a business proposal. Your own words were, 'this isn't a real marriage.' And now, now…you're expecting me to fall into the role as your wife." She shook her head, and her emotions spilled out. "Don't you understand? At one time, I would have trusted you with my life, but now there's not much you could say or do to make me trust you. My heart is empty where you're concerned. I was forced to marry you… otherwise I wouldn't be here. I'm protecting myself, and my baby."

"That's what *I* intend to do, Rena. Protect you and the baby."

"No, you're going to help build my company back up. Period. I can't let you get too close to my child. I can't let you hurt my baby, the way you hurt me."

"How could I ever hurt your child?"

"The same way you hurt me. By walking out. By

leaving. By finding something more exciting than being a husband and father. While I've recovered from you leaving, it would be devastating to a child to be abandoned that way. My son or daughter may never get over it."

Anger flashed in his eyes. His jaw tightened, and his body went rigid. "I don't intend on abandoning either of you."

"What if you get the racing bug again? What if you're called back? It's in your blood, Tony. You love racing."

"That part of my life is over. I did what I set out to do. I'm not going back, ever."

Rena shook her head, refusing to believe him.

"You have my promise on that," he said. Then he spoke more firmly. "Did you hear me, Rena? I'll never leave you or the baby. It's a promise."

Tony stared at her for a long moment, and when she thought he was so angry he'd walk out of the room, he handed her a plate. "Eat up," he said. "We're going to have some fun today."

Rena glanced at him. "We are?"

"Yeah, even if it kills me."

Rena chuckled, despite the tension in the room just seconds earlier. She had to hand it to Tony for lightening the mood. "That's not my intention."

"Can I bank on that?"

She shrugged as she filled up her plate. "Sure," she offered. "You can bank on that."

They exited the hotel, and because it was a glorious day, they decided to walk the crowded streets. A few times, Rena and Tony got separated in the onslaught of foot traffic, so he grabbed her hand and they strolled along that way, browsing through shops. When Rena took a lingering look at a ruby necklace, her birthstone with a setting that was beautifully unusual, Tony dragged her into the store and purchased it for her. "You don't have to do this," she said.

"Consider it a wedding gift, since I didn't get you a diamond ring."

"I know, but I don't need this. What I need is for my vineyard to thrive and be solvent again."

"That'll happen too, Rena. You don't have to give up one to get the other."

Rena sighed inwardly. She'd been doing that most of her life, sacrificing her own needs and wants in order to assure Purple Fields' survival. It had been years since she'd known what it was like to simply have something she wanted without guilt.

Next they took the trolley to Fisherman's Wharf and ate clam chowder in sourdough bread bowls, then stopped at an ice cream parlor and ate sundaes until Rena thought her belly would expand out of her pants. "Oh, I'm so full."

"Me, too," Tony said, looking at her empty dish. "I guess you never get over loving hot fudge over strawberry ice cream."

"With nuts on top."

"Hmm and whipped cream. Remember the whipped cream fight we had?" Tony asked.

Rena remembered how they'd each taken out a can of Reddi-wip from Tony's refrigerator. No one was home and they'd just finished eating sundaes. "Yeah and you cheated!"

"I did not. I fight fair. I couldn't help it that your nozzle got stuck."

"You took advantage then and squirted me until I was covered with it. That stuff even got in my hair."

"You were sweet from head to toe," Tony said with a nostalgic smile.

The memory popped into her head of Tony kissing it off her until kissing wasn't enough. He'd taken her to his bedroom then, stripped her down and licked every bit of the whipped cream off. They'd made love in the shower, deciding that strawberry sundaes were their favorite dessert.

"I never have whipped cream without thinking of you," Tony said, his eyes fixed on hers.

Her cheeks heated and she inhaled sharply. "That was a long time ago." What she didn't add is that the same held true for her.

"But a good memory."

"I don't think about the past anymore," she fibbed.

He watched her intently. "Maybe you should. We had something special."

"'Had' being the key word." She refused to let Tony get to her.

Tony leaned over and kissed her on the lips. "Let's go," he said abruptly, taking her hand again. They rode the trolley back and checked out of the hotel. Rena took one last look around, feeling oddly sentimental. She blamed it on her fickle hormones.

When Rena thought they'd head back to Napa, Tony

drove her to a four-story shopping mall and parked the car. "What are we doing here?"

He grinned. "We're getting baby things."

"Baby things?"

"I promised you a fun day, and I figured a new mother-to-be would enjoy picking out furniture and clothes and whatever else the baby might need."

"Really?" Tempted by such an elaborate offer, Rena's heart raced with excitement. Offhand, she could think of dozens of items she'd need for the baby's arrival, and quite frankly, she didn't know how she'd manage to pay for all of it. Other than shopping at thrift stores, she was truly at a loss.

"I haven't a clue what a baby needs," Tony said, getting out of the car and opening the door for her.

"I'm on new ground here, too." She took his outstretched hand. "We'd always talked about having children, but—" Rena stopped and slipped her hand from his, her heart in her throat. How could she do this? How could she look at cribs and bassinets and baby swings when this was a dream she and David shared together? They'd always wanted a family. The time had never been right. She refused to think of the life growing inside her as an accident, but they hadn't really planned on this baby.

Rena ached inside thinking that David would never know his child. He'd never change a diaper, kiss its face or watch it take its first step. He'd never go to a ballet recital or little league game. He'd never know the joy of seeing his child develop into a smart-alecky teen or fall in love one day. David would have been there for his child. He'd have seen his son or daughter through the good times and the bad, because David was loyal and devoted. He would have made a wonderful father.

Rena's legs went weak suddenly. Her body trembled, and she knew she couldn't do this. She glanced at Tony, her voice a quiet plea. "I'm sorry. I don't think I'm ready for this."

Tony drew in a breath. "Right." He closed his eyes briefly, and Rena noted genuine pain there. "Okay, we'll do this another time. When you're ready."

She sighed with relief. "It's not that I don't appreciate—"

"I get it, Rena. I'm not the baby's father. Enough said."

Tony got back into his car and revved the engine, waiting for her to climb inside. She bit her lip and held back tears as she sank into the car. They drove to Napa in silence, Rena glancing at Tony's stony expression every once in a while.

She knew in her head that David was gone. He was her past, while this angry man sitting beside her was her future.

The irony struck her anew.

How many times had she hoped to be Tony Carlino's wife? Only to find now she should have been more careful what she'd wished for.

Six

Tony drove to Napa, a debate going on in his head. On one hand, he knew Rena still grieved, but on the other hand, he'd taken responsibility for her. She was his wife now. He couldn't let her dictate the terms of their relationship, not if he planned to really honor David's dying wish. So he drove past Purple Fields and down the highway leading to his home.

"Where are we going?" she asked.

"To my house."

Rena slanted him a dubious look. "Why?"

"Just stopping by to pick up some of my clothes to bring to Purple Fields."

Rena blinked before realizing his intent. "This was supposed to be a secret marriage, Tony. We can't live together."

Tony expected this argument. He pulled to the side of the road and stopped the car. Immediately, Rena's shoulders stiffened. She sat up straighter in the seat and faced him. Before he spoke, he searched her face for a long moment, reining in his anger. "Rena, we're not announcing to the public we're married. But I can't possibly work with you at Purple Fields and—"

"Watch out for me," she finished for him with a twist of her full lips.

She tried his patience, but Tony held firm. He'd made up his mind about this and decided it was best for both of them. "We'll be discreet. Purple Fields isn't exactly bustling with crowds."

"Thanks for the reminder."

"Rena, listen. All I'm saying is that you don't have a big staff that will spread gossip through the county. The place isn't on the main highway. In fact, you're in a remote location."

Rena's voice held quiet concern, and she refused to look at him. "I didn't think we'd live together."

Tony reached over to gently turn her chin his way. She lifted those incredible eyes to him. "You're my wife. I'm your husband. We *are* married. We'll keep the secret for a while, but make no mistake that I intend for us to live as man and wife. Now, if you'd rather move into the Carlino estate with me, we can—"

"No!" She shook her head. "No, Tony. That makes no sense. I need to be at Purple Fields."

Tony wasn't fooled. Rena's hatred for his father was evident in her blatant refusal. After Tony had moved away, Santo Carlino had tried to ruin all the local vintners in the area, and Rudy Fairfield hadn't been the exception. Once Tony was gone, his father had ignored Tony's protests to leave Purple Fields alone. The Fairfields had suffered, but they'd never fully succumbed to his father's ruthless business tactics.

Rena hadn't stepped foot in his house since. It seemed his new wife hated *everything* Carlino.

"Well then, it's settled. I'll move into your house."

Rena swallowed and gave him a reluctant nod.

He bounded out of the car and opened her door. She looked up and announced, "I'll wait for you out here. It's a nice day. I need the...fresh air."

Tony didn't push her. He helped her out, making a mental note that his Porsche wasn't a family car or comfortable for his pregnant wife. "I'll be a few minutes."

She nodded and stretched out, raising her arms, shaking out the kinks, confirming that he'd been right about the car.

Tony bounded up the steps and entered the arched wrought iron doors decorated with delicate metal vines that led to a breezeway. The house, set more like an Italian villa atop the hill, had four wings that met in the center by a large expansive living room and dining area overlooking the vineyards. Tony liked his privacy, and each of the Carlino men had lived in separate sections of the house once they'd grown up.

"Hey, I thought I heard you come in. How are the newlyweds?" Joe asked, approaching him as he began his ascent up the stairs.

Tony sighed. "Fine."

"That bad? I take it the wedding night didn't go so smoothly."

Tony knew Joe meant well. He wasn't prying; he was simply concerned. "She's still grieving."

"Understandable. Where is she?"

"Outside. She won't come in. But I plan to rectify that soon. She's not thrilled that I'm moving in with her."

"I wasn't sure of your plans. I guess it makes sense for you to live there for a while."

"I'll divide my time between here and there, Joe, but I'd appreciate it if you and Nick could hold down the fort for a few days without me."

"Sure, no problem."

"Thanks. You know," he began with a slant of his head, "if you'd have told me six months ago I'd be married to Rena and raising a baby, I wouldn't have believed it."

"Am I hearing a little bit of awe in your voice?"

"Yeah, well, maybe I'm adjusting to the situation a little better than my wife is."

"She'll come around. In fact, I think I'll step outside and say hello to my new sister-in-law. Maybe put in a few good words for you."

"I can use all the help I can get. Rena thinks she married the devil." He chuckled as he took the steps up to his bedroom. He'd been called even worse by some of the women he'd dated in the past.

And it had all been true.

"Tony?" Rena questioned him immediately when she realized where they were going. Tony hadn't taken her directly back to Purple Fields after he'd picked up his clothes from his estate. Instead, he'd driven to the cemetery where David was buried.

"Are you okay with this?" he asked.

Rena squeezed her eyes shut. Right after David died, she'd made daily trips to the cemetery to lay wildflowers by his grave. She'd come and sit on the grass just to feel close to him again. But after she'd learned about the promise he'd asked of Tony, she'd gotten so angry with him for his manipulation that she hadn't come back since. Now she realized the folly in that. David had tried to protect her. Even in death, he'd tried to take care of her. Guilt assailed her for being so shortsighted and selfish. She should have come more often. She should have honored the man who'd loved her. "Yes, I'm okay with this."

Once out of the car, Tony met her on the lawn and put out his hand. She glanced down at it and then into his reassuring eyes. "We'll do this together."

She slipped her hand into his, and silently they walked to the center of the Gracious Hill section of the cemetery. A new bronze headstone with David's name and birth date embossed in gold stared up at them. Rena sank to her knees and said a prayer. She sat there for a minute, looking down, running her fingers over the headstone, touching David's nameplate with infinite care.

Tony helped her up, and taking her hand, he spoke with reverence as his gaze drifted down toward the grave. "She's safe, David," he whispered. "We're married now. I'll take good care of her."

Overwhelmed with emotion, Rena let out a sob. Tears she couldn't hold back, spilled down her cheeks. The reality of the last few weeks came crashing down on her.

"It's okay, honey," Tony said softly. He turned his body and encompassed her in his arms, cradling her as she cried into his chest. She sobbed deeply, the pain emanating from deep within. Guilt and sadness washed over her.

Tony tightened his hold on her. "Let it out, Rena."

Cocooned in Tony's strength and warmth, she cried and cried until she finally managed to control her emotions. She sniffed and gulped in oxygen and stopped crying after several minutes, yet she couldn't let go of Tony. Wrapped up in his arms, she was grateful for the comfort, the gentle assuring words, the soft kisses to her forehead. She gave herself up to Tony allowing him to be strong for her. She needed this. She needed for once to let someone else take the brunt of her heartache.

"He's okay with this, Rena," Tony whispered. "It's what David wanted."

She knew that to be true. But she also realized she had just married a man who had hurt and betrayed her once—a man whom she blamed for her husband's death, a man who'd felt obligated to marry her. How could she find comfort in that?

"I was mad at David for asking this of you. Of me," she whispered painfully. "I haven't come here in weeks."

Tony stroked her back again and again, keeping her head pressed to his chest. "Don't beat yourself up, Rena.

You're a strong woman, but you have a right to all your feelings."

"Even the ones that scream I shouldn't have married you?"

Tony looked down into her eyes. "Yeah, even those."

"I don't intend on cutting you any slack," she said quietly.

"Planning on making my life miserable?"

"Not deliberately, Tony. But yes. You may want to move out before the week is over."

"Doubtful. I'm not going anywhere."

Then he leaned down and kissed her softly, exquisitely on her lips, and for the first time, Rena came close to believing him.

With arms folded, Rena watched Tony set his bags on the floor beside her bed. He faced her, his gaze direct and piercing. "I told you, I won't tiptoe around you anymore. We're going to live as man and wife."

Rena drew in a breath. Exhausted, she had no more tears to shed. She'd used up her quota and then some at the cemetery. Though her insides quaked and her head ached, she knew she had no choice but to accept Tony in her home and in her bed. He had pride. He was virile and strong and extremely sexy. She suspected women had thrown themselves at him all the time. He was a race car champion, an appealing bachelor who was definitely easy on the eyes. He'd probably had women in every town he traveled.

Though he'd been patient and kind to her the past few

days she knew she'd pushed him pretty far. And soon, he'd start pushing back.

He must have noted her fear, because his jaw clenched and he swore. "For God's sake, Rena. I'm not about to force myself on you. But we will sleep in the same bed."

Rena glanced at the bed, then up at him. "I understand."

"Ah, hell." He rolled his eyes at her robotic answer. "You'd think we'd never had sex before. Mind-blowing, earthmoving, do-it-until-we-can't-breathe-anymore sex."

Rena nearly tripped over her own feet backing up, his statement stunning her. Her face heated, and her body shook a little. Speechless, she lowered her lashes, fighting off memories of their lovemaking. He'd been blunt but accurate in his description. "That's when…" she began, almost unable to get the words out. "When we were in love."

"Right." Tony tossed his overnight bag on the bed. He pulled out aftershave lotion, deodorant, razors and a hairbrush. "You have a place I can put these?"

She pointed to the master bathroom. "It's small, but you should find some room on the counter."

She'd taken David's things out of the bedroom, unwilling to have that daily reminder of his absence. But she'd yet to remove his clothes from the closet. She'd be forced to now. Tony would need the room, and unlike his home with massive walk-in closet space, her closets were barely big enough for two people.

She held out hope that he'd get disgusted with her

small three-bedroom house and move back to the estate where he'd be ensconced in luxury.

Rena opened her closet and began gathering up David's clothes to make room for Tony's. Before she knew it, Tony stood beside her and placed a stopping hand on hers. "You don't have to do it now. You're exhausted."

"It needs doing. I just never could fa—"

"If it makes you feel better, I'll do it."

"No," she said with a shake of her head. "I should do it."

Tony grabbed both of her hands while they were still on the hangers. He stood close. So close that she noted the golden flecks in his dark eyes. "Okay but not today. It can wait. Agreed?"

She nodded, breathing in his subtle, musky scent. A lump formed in her throat thinking of his stirring kiss before. She didn't want to be attracted to Tony. She'd gotten over him a long time ago, yet when he touched her or looked deep into her eyes or kissed her, emotions rolled around inside. And made her nervous. "I'll make dinner."

"Thank you."

She strode out of the room, confused by what she was feeling and angry for feeling anything at all.

Rena stirred the spaghetti sauce, watching as little bubbles broke on the surface sending a pungent, garlic scent into the air.

"Smells great." Tony came up behind her, his body close again, surprising her in how quietly he appeared in her kitchen. He reached for the wooden spoon. "May I?"

She handed it to him. "I hope you don't mind pasta tonight."

"Are you kidding? I'm Italian. You know I love pasta." He stirred the sauce, then lifted the spoon to his mouth, tasting it.

"What do you think?"

"Needs a little salt," he said, then grabbed the salt shaker and added a few shakes. "There."

"You like to cook, don't you?"

He shrugged. "I get by. When a bachelor wants to eat, he's got to know more than how to boil water."

"I didn't think you'd ever have to cook a meal for yourself."

Tony continued stirring the sauce. "When my gourmet chef was off, I had three other servants waiting on me hand and foot." He turned to her and grinned.

"You're teasing."

"Yeah, I'm teasing." Then he set the wooden spoon down and stared at her. "I'm not going to apologize for how I live. I've earned it. Racing has afforded me a good life. But there were sixteen-hour work days, long lonely times on the road. Times when I had to cook for myself when I longed for a home cooked meal. Eating out is overrated."

"There must have been plenty of women happy to cook for you. Never mind," Rena said, catching herself. She didn't really want to know. "Forget I said that."

Tony's expression changed, and he gave her a quick shake of the head. "Your image of me is way off."

Rena pursed her lips. "It really doesn't matter."

Tony grabbed her arms gently as steam rose up from the sauce and bathed them in heat. "Yes, it does matter. I'm your husband. I care what you think of me."

Rena stared into his eyes, unable to answer. She had mixed emotions when it came to Tony Carlino, but for the most part, she didn't want to see any good in him. She wanted to keep him a safe distance away in her mind and heart.

When he realized she wouldn't respond, he let her go and she went about filling a big pot of water for the pasta noodles.

Tony watched her work at the stove for a long while before he spoke again. "What can I do to help?"

Grateful to give him something to do, she barked orders. "Take out the romaine and tomatoes from the refrigerator. I think there's a cucumber in there, too— and anything else you can find for a salad."

She heard him going to work, and much to her surprise, he fixed a delicious salad, and, adding black olives and herbs, he made his own olive oil-based dressing.

When she walked over to taste it, she cast him a nod of approval. "Yummy."

"My mother's. One of a few recipes I learned from her before she died."

Tony's mother died when he was fifteen. Rena hadn't known her, but she'd heard she was a saint among women. She'd have to be in order to be married to Santo Carlino. Rumor had it she'd kept him in line. When she died, Santo poured himself into building his business taking no prisoners along the way.

"And you remembered it," Rena said. "It's funny the things we remember about the ones we love."

"What do you remember about your mother?" he asked.

Rena smiled wide, recalling her mother's favorite pastime. "That's easy. She had a morning and nightly ritual of walking three miles. No matter how tired she was, no matter the weather. She'd get into her walking clothes, put on these beat-up old shoes and go for a walk. She said it cleared the mind, cleansed the soul and kept the weight off." Rena grinned, confessing. "My mama liked to eat."

Tony chuckled. "That's a good way to remember her. Walking, I mean. Not eating."

"Hmm, yeah." Rena blinked herself back to reality. Even with all her exercise, her mother still contracted a deadly disease. She'd lingered for years, missing her daily walks and everything else that required a bit of effort. It was a brutal reminder of the unfairness in life.

Once the meal was ready, they sat down to eat at her country oak kitchen table. She wondered what Tony thought about this rustic house. To her it was home, and she wasn't ashamed of it. Through the years, she'd put personal touches throughout, cheerful curtains, comfy sofas with throw pillows she'd sewn, refinished tables, armoires and cabinets. When she looked around her home, she saw bits and pieces of her parents' life here as well as her life with David.

Facing Tony at her kitchen table reminded her once again how it had all changed so quickly.

Tony ate up heartily. There would be no salad-only dinners for him. He was a well-built man who enjoyed a good meal. He was halfway through a large dish of pasta when he lifted his head. "I want to see your accounts tomorrow. I hope to get through them by the end of the week. Then I'll know better how we can get your winery back on track."

Grateful that he'd taken the first step, Rena discussed with him her conversation she had with the banker. Tony hadn't even blinked when she told him her financial situation and how much money she owed.

"I'll take care of it," he said, without pause. "You'll make your payroll, and any other debts you have will be dealt with."

"Thank you." Humbled by his generosity, she put her head down.

"Rena?" She looked up into his dark eyes. "We're in this together from now on. You don't have to worry about the winery."

"I know. I appreciate everything, really. I just can't help feeling like a failure. I tried. David tried. We had some bad luck, equipment that needed replacing, problems with distributors and well, the bigger wineries tried to shove us out."

Tony covered her hand, and the instant spark jolted her. "Carlino Wines being one of them. That's not going to happen anymore."

She tried to ignore sensations rippling through her. "The Fairfields have always taken pride in their livelihood. *I* have a lot of pride. I feel like I let my parents down. I had to remarry to save the business."

Tony stroked her hand, his fingers caressing hers. It felt good—too good—to pull her hand away. Lord help her, she needed to feel his touch.

"I won't take offense to that," he said. "I know I'm the last person on earth you'd want as a husband."

She watched as his fingers slid over her knuckles so gently. "At one time, I wanted nothing more."

"And now?"

She gazed deeply into his eyes and lifted a shoulder in confusion. "Now, I don't know, Tony. I really don't know. I'm just so tired."

Tony rose from the table with concern in his eyes. "Go. I'll take care of this." He took up their plates and headed toward the dishwasher. "You need to rest. It's been a long day."

Rena got up, ready to argue, but Tony had already rinsed their dishes and began loading them into the dishwasher. With his back to her, she noted his broad shoulders tapering down along his back and slim waistline. His slacks fit perfectly over his buttocks, and she recalled the quick flash of excitement she felt when he'd stepped out of the shower yesterday, buck naked. She'd only caught a glimpse, but oh, that image wouldn't leave her anytime soon.

"I, uh, thanks. I'll take a quick shower and go to bed. What will you—"

He turned sharply and met her gaze. "I'll come to bed later, Rena."

She gave him a clipped nod, turned around and strode

out of the room. Her exhaustion catching up with her, she was too tired to think of the implications of sleeping with her new, extremely sexy secret husband.

Seven

Rena snuggled deeper into her bed, rebelling against thin rays of dawn creeping into the room. She closed her eyes tighter, rolling away from the light and into familiar warmth. Cocooned in the heat now, she relaxed and let out a stress-relieving sigh.

Her eyelids blessedly shut, she breathed in a pleasing musky scent and smiled. A warm breath brushed her cheek, then another and another. She popped her eyes open. Tony was there, inches from her face, his eyes dark and dusky. He lay stretched out on his side, apparently watching her sleep. "Morning, beautiful."

Alarm bells rang out in her head. She couldn't believe she was in bed with Tony. And enjoying it. His warmth surrounded her. She focused on the firm set of his sculpted jaw, then opened her mouth to speak, but

Tony placed his finger to her lips, stopping her words. "Shh. Don't overthink this, Rena." He wrapped his arms around her waist and drew her closer.

She remembered putting on her most unappealing nightshirt last night, a soft, brushed cotton garment with tiny cap sleeves just in case Tony held true to his word to sleep with her. But Rena liked to feel feminine in bed, so the least suggestive nightgown she owned was still a far cry from head-to-toe flannel.

"Don't overthink what?"

"This," he said, moving closer and touching his lips to hers. The heat of his mouth and the intimate contact should have caused her to panic. Yet, she didn't resist, her body and mind not fully operational at the moment. He pulled away long enough to search her eyes and must have been satisfied with what he saw in them.

Tony knew how to kiss a woman, and he held nothing back with the next kiss. He drew her in with expert finesse, coaxing a reaction from her. His hand on her waist, she felt his strength through the thin cotton fabric of the nightgown. He squeezed her gently, and immediate tingles coursed through her body. She sighed aloud, a throaty little sound that emanated from deep within. Tony moved his hand up, stroking her side slowly up and down, his fingers brushing the underside of her breast.

Oh God, it felt good to have him caress her, teasing her breast until she ached for his touch.

Rena loved the physical act of making love. She loved the intimacy, the joy of having her body succumb to infinite pleasure. Tony had taught her that. He'd taken her virginity and taught her to enjoy sexual intercourse. Of course, back then they'd been so much in love that holding back wasn't an option. She'd given herself fully to him, surrendering her heart and her body. She'd only been with two men in her life, and each in their own way had taught her about loving a man. Where David had been sweet, patient and dependable, Tony had been irresistible, hot-blooded and sexy.

Tony's passionate kisses unnerved her. His touch drew her like a magnet. She moved closer, arching toward him, her breaths heavier now. He nibbled on her lips, whispering how beautiful she was, how much he wanted to touch her.

She gave him permission with a sigh.

His hand came up and cupped her breast over the fabric of her cotton nightie. He flicked a finger over the tip, rubbing back and forth, sending shock waves through her body. Intense heat swamped her, and she longed for more.

She knew the instant Tony's body went taut. His breaths deepened, and his kisses became more demanding as he parted her lips. His tongue beckoned hers, and she met him halfway. They sparred in an endless search for satisfaction.

While her body craved the physical release, her heart and mind screamed no. Torn by indecision, she stilled, forcing herself to think this through.

"You're overthinking again, Rena," Tony said in a low rasp. He continued to stroke her breast, unraveling her mind.

She mustered her willpower and covered his hand with hers, stopping him. "One of us has to."

"I told you I don't plan on being celibate in this marriage," he said quietly. "If I thought you weren't ready, I'd back off. But the woman I was just kissing wasn't protesting at all. You were enjoying having my hands on you. In another second I would have taken off your nightgown, and we would have been skin to skin. I want that, and I know you want that, too."

Rena's heart pumped hard. He was right, but she had to voice her innermost thoughts. "Wanting and having are two different things."

"Rena's rules, not mine."

Rena drew oxygen in. "I can't forget who you are. I can't ignore what you did to me. My heart is empty where you're concerned."

"So you've said." Tony flopped onto his back and looked at the ceiling. "What's done is done, Rena. I can't change that."

"I know. And I can't change how I feel. I may want you physically, but you'll never really have me. I can't love you again. I won't. You'll never own my heart."

"As long as you're faithful to me, that's all I'll ask for now."

Stunned by the statement, Rena lifted her head off the pillow. "You know me, Tony. I'd never even consider—"

He turned onto his side again to face her. "What you don't know about me is that I'd never consider it, either. But I'm a man with physical needs, and since we're married and compatible in bed, there's no reason not to make love."

"You mean, *have sex?* Because without love, it's just sex," Rena pointed out.

He lifted a strand of her hair, eyeing it as he let it fall from his fingers. "Just sex?" Tony cocked her a playful grin. "Even better."

Rena shook her head in bewilderment.

"C'mon, Rena. We've cleared the air. I get it. You don't love me, but you crave my body."

"I never said that!"

"Oh, no?" he said innocently. He was such a tease. He crushed his mouth to hers and kissed her passionately. She'd hardly come up for air when he grabbed her hand and set it on his chest. "Touch me."

Crisp scattered hairs filled her palm and underneath muscles rippled. She wove her hand up along his sculpted shoulders then down to tease his flattened nipple. His intake of air let her know he enjoyed her flicking her finger over him, the way he had to her.

Laying her hand against his torso, she inched her way down, tempted by a perfect body and powered by the sounds of Tony's quick jagged breaths. Okay, so maybe she did crave his body. She had memories that wouldn't go away. Sexual flashes that entered her mind at the most inopportune times. She'd remembered how he'd made her feel, how potent his lovemaking was, how satisfied she'd been afterward. If anything, Tony had matured into a stunning male specimen. He knew how to give pleasure, and he knew how to take it. He'd always made Rena feel special and cherished, no matter what act they performed.

She slid her hand farther down, slipping below Tony's waistline. When she reached the elastic band of his boxers, she hesitated, tentative in her approach. Myriad thoughts flitted through her mind one right after the other, but Tony interrupted that train of thought. "Just let go, Rena," he whispered. "We both need this."

Rena touched him then, her hand gliding over silken skin. His arousal shocked her, though she didn't know why it should. He was a virile man, and they were in bed together, ready to consummate their marriage.

"I want you." Tony's low tone held no room for doubt. He cupped her chin and brought her lips to his. There was a sense of urgency to his kiss, yet he remained gentle and patient, waiting for her to respond. She stroked him with trebling fingers, bringing him to a fuller state of arousal.

"This is not—" Rena began, but Tony kissed her again, his mouth generous and giving, coaxing her to fulfill their destiny. Torn by indecision, she shoved all thoughts of the past years aside and tried to focus on the future.

"We'll have a life together, Rena." Tony's words mirrored her own. Her life included him now, whether planned or not, whether she liked it or not. She had no other option now.

"I know," she said, finally resigning to her fate.

Tony removed his boxers then placed her hand back on him, skin to skin, and her insides turned to jelly. There was life to Tony, a vitality she'd missed during these past months. He filled the void, the hollowness that beseeched her since she'd become a widow. She had her precious child, yes, but this intimacy fulfilled her need to feel alive again.

She stroked him until his pleasure heightened. Instincts, or perhaps recollection, told her that he'd reached his limit. He flipped her onto her back, and in one quick sweep, he removed her nightgown, pulling it up and over her head. His kisses burned her through and through, and his hands roamed over her, touching, tormenting, caressing and teasing every inch of her skin. His voice was low and consumed with passion. "You're as beautiful as I remember."

He brought his mouth down to suckle her breast, his tongue wetting her with long swipes. After laving each nipple, he blew on them, and every ounce of her body prickled with need. Her pulse raced with exquisite excitement. Unmindful of any repercussions, she relished the thrill of the moment.

Tony praised her body with quiet expletives and cherished every limb before moving on to touch her at the apex of her legs. His palm covered her, and she arched up.

"You're ready for me, sweetheart," he acknowledged. Without hesitation, he rose over her. She gazed up at him, and images of their past, of doing this very thing with nothing but love in their hearts, played out in her mind. She'd relished their joining, eager to show the man she loved how much he meant to her. It had been perfect. Blissful. Exciting.

Tony stared into her eyes in the dawn light, and she

witnessed that same spark. The memories had come back to him, as well. His lips lifted and his eyelids lowered. Then he gripped her hips and she squeezed her eyes shut, ready for him to take her.

"Look at me," he commanded.

"Tony," she murmured, popping her eyes open. It was clear what he wanted. No memories of any other man. No memories of David.

He nodded when their eyes met, apparently satisfied, then he moved inside her with extreme care. Rena adjusted to his size and accommodated him with her body. It wasn't long before his thrusts magnified, their bodies sizzled hot and the burn she'd remembered from long ago returned fiercely.

Infinitely careful and recklessly wild, Tony made love to her, seeing to her needs, giving as much as taking, gentle at times and feral at others. He was the perfect lover—that much hadn't changed. And all the while, Rena gave up her body to him but held firmly onto her emotions.

It was *just sex*.

And as Tony brought her to the peak of enjoyment, her skin damp, her body throbbing for the release that would complete her, she wrapped her arms around his neck and arched up, her bones melting but her heart firmly intact.

Tony wrapped Rena in his arms. They lay quietly together on the bed after making love, each deep in thought. It had been months since he'd had sex, and his release had come with powerful force. Rena had responded to him as she always had, with wild abandon. At least her body had reacted as he'd hoped. He knew what she liked and how to please her. She'd been his first love, too, and a man doesn't easily forget how to please the woman he loves.

They'd been so young back then, full of dreams and plans for the future. But Tony had been a rebel. He'd hated being under his father's thumb. He hadn't wanted any part of the family business, not when racing cars meant so much to him. He'd never planned on leaving Rena behind. It just happened. While his professional life had been great, his personal life had suffered.

Once he'd become a champion, he had women knocking at his door at all hours of the night. They followed him from race to race. They'd called him, showed up when he least expected it. Beautiful, sexy, outrageous women. He'd never fallen in love with any of them. He'd had flings and a few casual relationships that never lasted more than a couple of months.

He'd held hope for Rena in the early years, but he hadn't blamed her for giving up on him. He hadn't known what the future held for him other than racing cars. He was on the road a great deal of time, thrilled by his success but heartbroken about Rena.

His gaze fell to Rena's face, her expression glum, her eyes filled with regret. Hardly the loving wife in the aftermath of lovemaking.

Hell, he felt like crap himself, guilt eating at him. He wanted to do right by David, but he couldn't forget that a few months ago, his friend was alive and well and living with the woman he loved. He was to become a father, something that David always wanted.

Tony had suspected David had feelings for Rena early on. They had been good friends in school, yet all three understood in an unspoken agreement that Rena and Tony were meant for each other. When Tony left town, David stayed behind to pick up the pieces of Rena's shattered heart. He'd loved her that much to forego a chance to enter the racing circuit with Tony. To Rena's way of thinking, David was her white knight coming to her rescue, where Tony was the villain who'd abandoned her.

Now they'd consummated a loveless marriage.

Her remorse irritated him more than it should. Was it ego on his part? They'd just made incredible love, and now Rena looked so darn miserable.

Damn it, what did she expect? She was his wife. He would raise her child as his own. They'd both agreed to honor David's last wishes. That meant living as man and wife and sleeping together. He blinked away anger and guilt then rose abruptly, mindless of his state of undress. "I'll grab a shower, then I want to go over your accounts."

Rena glanced at him for an instant, bit down on her lip then focused her attention out the window. "I'll make breakfast."

"I'm not hungry," he said. "Coffee will do. Meet me in the office once you're dressed."

Rena nodded without looking at him.

Tony showered quickly and dressed with clothes he'd taken from his bag. He put on a pair of faded jeans and a black T-shirt then shoved his feet into a pair of seasoned white Nike shoes.

He heard kitchen sounds as he walked down the hallway, the aroma of hot coffee brewing, whetting his taste buds. But instead of greeting his new wife in the kitchen, he strode outside and closed the door. The northern California air was crisp and fresh, the brilliant sky laced with white puffy clouds.

He filled his lungs several times, breathing in and out slowly, enjoying the pristine air. The vineyards were far removed from the city, elevated to some degree, the vistas spread out before him, glorious. Funny, as a young boy, he'd had no appreciation for the land or its beauty and solitude. He'd never seen this country as his father had seen it.

Now he'd make a life here. The irony that his father was getting what he wanted in death, rather than in life, was never far from his mind.

Tony entered the office adjacent to the gift shop with the key Rena had left for him on her dresser. He glanced around, noting two tall file cabinets, an outdated computer, a desk that had seen better days and shelves displaying certificates, wine awards and pictures of Rena and David. He walked over and picked one up that was encased in a walnut frame. He looked at the image of the couple standing among the vines ripe with cabernet grapes.

"It was a good year for cabernet. Our fifth anniversary." Rena walked into the office with a cup of coffee and set it down on the desk.

Tony stared at the photo. "You look happy."

"David made me dinner that night. He set up twinkling lights out on the patio. We danced in the moonlight."

Tony put the frame back, deciding not to comment. What could he say to that? "Thanks for the coffee."

She shrugged. "Well, this is the office. Our accounts for the past ten years are in those file cabinets."

Tony picked up the coffee cup and sipped. The liquid went down hot and delicious, just what he needed. "I'll start with the past year and work my way backward."

"Okay, I'll get those for you."

"Are they all paper files? Do you have anything loaded into the computer?"

Rena glanced at the machine. "We have our inventory computerized now. And David had started to enter the paper files. But he didn't get very far, I'm afraid."

Tony sat down at the desk and signed on. "Want to show me where everything is?"

Rena came close, her hair still slightly damp from her shower. She bent over the computer, clicking keys. Her clean scent wafted in the air. "What is that?" he asked.

She looked at him in question. "What?"

"You smell great."

She smiled softly. "It's citrus shampoo."

Tony met her eyes, then took her hand gently. "Rena... listen, about this morning."

She squeezed her eyes shut and shook her head. "Don't, Tony. I can't help how I feel."

"How *do* you feel?"

She hesitated for a moment, but Tony fixed his gaze

on her and wouldn't back down. She sighed quietly. "Like I sold my soul."

"To the devil?"

Her lips tightened as if holding back a comment.

Tony leaned in his chair, releasing her hand. "Physically, are you okay?"

"Yes," she said. "I'm fine. I see the doctor next week, but I'm healthy."

She continued clicking on keys, showing him where the files were kept and how to access them. Then she came upon a document and lingered, her gaze drawn to the words on the screen: *Vine by Vine*. "Don't worry about this," she said, her finger on the delete button.

"Wait." Tony stopped her. "What is it?"

"It's nothing." Rena said, but he wouldn't let it go. Something in her eyes told him, whatever it was, it was important to her.

"I need to see everything, Rena. If I'm going to help you."

"It's got nothing to do with the accounts, Tony. Trust me."

"So why won't you let me see it?" Determined, he pressed her.

"Oh, for heaven's sake!" Rena straightened, her eyes sparkling like blue diamonds. "It's just a story I was writing."

"A *story?*" That sparked his curiosity. "What's it about?"

"It's about a girl growing up in the wine country."

"It's about you?"

"No, it's a novel. It's fiction, but yes, I guess some

of it is about what I know and how I feel about living here. It's sort of a wine guide but told from a different perspective. It's an analogy of how a girl grows to womanhood—"

"And you relate that to how a vine grows? Sort of like, how you need to be cared for and loved and nourished."

"Yeah," she said, her expression softening. "Something like that."

"You're not finished with it?"

She made a self-deprecating sound. "No, I'd forgotten about it. There's too much to do around here." She shrugged it off. "I never found the time."

"Maybe someday you'll have time to finish it."

Rena stared deeply into his eyes. "Right now, I'm more interested in saving my winery."

Tony glanced at the computer screen, satisfied that she'd removed her finger from the delete button. "Agreed. That's the first order of business. We have to find a way to keep Purple Fields afloat."

Rena walked into the gift shop through a door adjacent to the office, leaving Tony to work his magic on their books. She'd given him all the files, answered his questions and left once he was neck-deep in the accounts, unaware of her presence any longer.

Her small little haven of trinkets and boutique items always perked up her spirits. She loved setting up the displays, making each unique object stand out and look desirable to the customer. They made very little profit on the shop, but it complimented the wine-tasting room and made the whole area look appealing.

Rena sighed with relief rather than anguish this time. For so long she'd had the burden of saving Purple Fields on her shoulders, and the weight had become unbearably heavy. Now she knew that with Tony's assets backing her up she had salvaged the future of Purple Fields, thus insuring her baby's future as well. She could only feel good about that.

But saving the winery had come at a high price. If it weren't for the promise she made to David, she wondered if she'd be standing here right now. She'd been set to sell Purple Fields and move away, making a fresh start with her child. Now she was tied to Tony Carlino, and the notion prickled her nerves.

She didn't want to enjoy being in his arms this morning. She didn't want to admit that having sex with him made her world spin upside down. She *hated* that she'd liked it. That she'd responded to him the way she always had. Tony wasn't a man easily forgotten, but she'd managed it for twelve years. Now he was back in her life and planned to stay.

Solena entered the gift shop, thankfully interrupting her thoughts. "Hey, you're up and out early this morning."

Rena smiled at her friend, happy to see her. "It's just another workday."

Solena eyed her carefully. "Is it? I thought you got married two days ago."

"Seems longer," Rena said, lifting her lips at her little joke.

"That bad?"

Rena glanced at the door leading to the office. "I shouldn't complain. He's in there right now, going over all our files and accounts. He's owning up to his end of the bargain."

Solena walked behind the counter and spoke with concern and sympathy. "Are you doing the same, my friend?"

Rena lowered her lashes. "I'm trying. I'm really trying. I never thought we'd live together like this. We, uh—" Heat reached her cheeks, and she realized she'd blushed, something she rarely did.

Solena spoke with understanding. "Tony's a very handsome, appealing man, Rena."

"So was David." Tears welled in her eyes.

Solena leaned over the counter to take her hands. Rena absorbed some of her strength through the solid contact. "David is the past, Rena. As hard as that is to hear, it's true. You have to look forward, not back."

"But I feel so…guilty."

Solena held firm. "Remind yourself that David wanted this."

"There are times when I really hate Tony," she whispered. "And I'm ashamed that I'm not too thrilled with David for making me do this."

"But we both know why he did."

Rena tilted her head to one side. "There's more. I should have told you sooner."

"What?" Solena's dark eyes narrowed with concern.

Rena hesitated, staring at her friend. Finally she blurted, "I'm pregnant."

Solena drew in a big breath then let it go in relief. "Oh! You had me scared for a second there, imagining the worst." Quickly, she walked around the counter to give Rena a hug. "This is good news...really good news."

"Yes, it is. I know." A tear dropped down her cheek. She'd already fallen in love with her baby. "I'm happy about the baby, but now do you see why I'm so, so—"

"You're torn up inside. I can see that. But you have hope and a new life to bring into this world. Oh Rena, my dear friend, I couldn't be happier for you."

She glanced at the office door and lowered her voice, speaking from the heart. "David should raise his child, not Tony."

Solena's eyes softened with understanding. "But that can't be. Your feeling bad isn't going to change that. It takes a remarkable man to raise another man's child. Tony knows?"

"He knows."

"You resent him."

"Yes, I do. I resent him for so many reasons. I'm so afraid."

"Afraid?" Solena met her gaze directly. "You're afraid of Tony?"

She shook her head. "No, not of him. Of me. I'm afraid I'll forgive him. I don't want to forget the hurt and pain he caused me. I don't want to ever forgive him."

Tony spent the morning loading the Purple Fields files into a new database program. His first order of business was to update the computer. He wasn't a genius at business like his brother Joe, but he knew the value of state-of-the-art equipment. Rena needed a new computer, but for now he'd do what he could and download everything to a flash drive.

Rena walked into the office holding a plate of food. "It's after one, and you haven't eaten lunch."

Tony glanced at his watch, then leaned back in his seat. "I didn't realize the time."

She set the plate down onto the desk. "Ham and cheese. I have chicken salad made if you'd prefer that instead?"

Tony grabbed the sandwich and took a bite. "This is fine," he said, his stomach acknowledging the late hour. "Did you eat?"

"Solena and I had a bite earlier. Since David's death, she's been babysitting me. She thinks I don't know it, but it's sweet. We usually have lunch together."

"What about Ray?"

"He eats a huge breakfast at home and skips lunch."

"Do you have time to sit down?" he asked. "I could use the company."

He rose from his chair, offering it to her. He waited until she took the seat before he sat on the edge of the desk, stretching his legs out. He wasn't used to poring over a computer screen for hours. He wasn't used to being holed up behind a desk in a small office either.

He gobbled his sandwich and began working on the apple she'd cut into wedges. "How's your day going?"

"Good," she said. "I gave a wine tour at eleven, and we sold a few cases today. Want something to drink?"

"I'll have a beer later. I'll need it."

She tilted her head, her pretty blue eyes marked with question. "Too many numbers?"

"Yeah. I'm inputting files. Setting up a database. My eyes are crossing."

She laughed. "I know what you mean."

Tony liked the sound of her laughter. He stared at a smile that lit the room. "You do?"

"All those numbers can make you crazy."

He grinned. "I think I'm there now." He gobbled up the apple wedges. "Thanks for lunch."

Rena watched him carefully. "You're welcome."

"You need a new computer and some stuff for the office. This thing is outdated. We'll work out a time to do that."

Rena's eyes widened. "A new computer? I, uh, we never could afford—"

"I know," Tony said softly. "But now we can."

"And you need me for that?"

"Yes, I need your input. Look, we can drive into the next town if you'd feel more comfortable, but—"

"I would." She offered without hesitation.

Tony's ego took a nosedive. He'd promised her a secret marriage and he'd stick to it, but he wasn't accustomed to women not wanting to be seen with him. Usually, it was just the opposite—women enjoyed being seen around town with him.

Irritated now, he agreed. "Fine."

"So what are your plans?" She stood and picked up his empty plate.

"I loaded the info to a flash drive. I'm going to have Joe take a look at everything. Though I have my suspicions, I need his opinion."

"You're going home tonight?"

Her hope-filled voice only irritated him some more. With legs spread, he reached out and pulled her between them, the plate separating their bodies. "Yeah, but I'll be back." He kissed her soundly on the lips reminding her of the steamy way they'd made love early this morning. He nuzzled her neck, and the devil in him added with a low rasp, "I have more inputting to do."

Rena's eyes snapped up to his.

He smiled and then released her.

He'd told her no more tiptoeing around and he'd meant it.

Eight

Tony entered the Carlino offices, a two-story building set in the heart of Napa Valley. The older outer structure gave way to a modern, innovative inner office filled with leather and marble. The mortar and stone building had been classified as a ghost winery, once owned by an aging retired sea captain who had run the place in the 1890s until Prohibition put him out of business, along with nearly seven hundred other wineries in the area. While some wineries had been turned into estates and restaurants, some held true to their original destiny, haunted not by ghostly spirits but by the passage of time and ruin.

The place had lain dormant and in a state of wreckage until Santo Carlino purchased the property then renovated it into their office space.

Tony walked into the reception area and was greeted by a stunningly gorgeous redhead. "Hi, you must be Tony Carlino." The woman—her cleavage nearly spilling out of her top—lifted up from her desk to shake his hand. "Joe said you'd be stopping by. I'm Alicia Pendrake, but you can call me Ali."

"Hi, Ali." He grasped her hand and shook.

"I'm Joe's new personal assistant. Today's my second day on the job."

"Nice to meet you," Tony said, curious why Joe didn't mention hiring anyone new when they spoke, especially one who looked like an overly buxom supermodel, with rich auburn curls draping over her shoulders, wearing a sleek outfit and knee-high boots.

She pointed to the main office door. "He's inside, crunching numbers, what else?"

Tony chuckled. The woman was a spitfire. "Okay, thanks."

"Nice meeting you, Mr. Carlino."

"It's Tony."

"Okay, Tony." She granted him a pleased smile that sent his male antenna up.

He found Joe seated behind his desk, staring at the computer screen. He made sure to close the door behind him. "Whoa...where did you find her?"

"Find who?" Joe said, his attention focused on the computer.

"Alicia...Ali. Your new PA."

Joe's brows furrowed and he took off his glasses, rubbing his eyes. "I met her in New York last year. She's efficient and capable."

"I bet. What happened to Maggie?"

"I had to let her go. She wasn't doing her job. This place was in chaos when I got here. I remembered Ali, and I called her. Offered to pay her way out here, gave her an advance on her salary to get set up. I didn't think she'd take the job."

"But she did. Just like that?"

"Yeah, I got lucky."

"*You got lucky?* Joe, the woman is beyond gorgeous. Haven't you noticed?"

Joe rubbed his jaw. "She's attractive, I suppose."

"You suppose? Maybe you need better glasses."

"My glasses are fine. I'm not interested, Tone. You know that I've sworn off women. After what happened with Sheila, I'm basically immune to beautiful women… to all women actually. Ali is smart. She's dedicated, and she does her work without complaint. She's very organized. You know how I am about organization."

Tony's lips twitched. "Okay, if you say so."

"So, what's up? You said you needed a favor?"

Tony tossed the flash drive onto the desk. "I need you to compare these accounts from Purple Fields with ours, for the same dates. I've been going over Rena's books. I just need your expert opinion."

"How soon?"

"Today?"

"I can do that." Joe inserted the flash drive into his computer. "I'll upload the files and let you know what I find out."

"Great, oh and can you burn them to a CD for me? There's something else I want to check on."

"Sure thing. I'll do that first."

While Joe burned the information to a disk, Tony walked around the office, noting the subtle changes Joe had made to Santo Carlino's office. Joe had secured even more high tech equipment than his father had used and updated the phone system. He was determined to make the company paperless, sooner rather than later.

It would seem that the only thing left from the older generation of the winery were the vast acres of vineyards—six hundred in all—the grapes that couldn't be digitalized into growing faster and the wine itself.

After a few minutes, Joe handed him a CD of Rena's accounts. "Here you go."

Tony tapped the CD against his palm. "Thanks."

"So how's married life?"

Tony shrugged, wishing he knew the answer to that question. "Too soon to tell. I'll be back later. You don't have plans tonight, do you?"

Joe shook his head. "Just work."

"Okay, I'll see you around six."

Tony walked out of the office after bidding farewell to Ali, who was as intent on her computer screen as Joe had been. He drove out of town and up the hills to the Carlino estate, waving a quick hello to Nick as he drove off the property with a pretty woman in his car. Tony only shook his head at his happy-go-lucky brother, thinking "been there, done that."

Tony entered the house and grabbed a beer out of the refrigerator. Taking a big swig from the bottle, he walked upstairs to his quadrant of the house, entered his private office and sat down at his desk. He logged onto his computer and inserted the CD into the slot.

He stopped for one moment, contemplating what he was about to do. Taking another gulp of beer, he sighed with indecision, but his curiosity got the better of him. He searched the files and finally found what he'd been looking for. The screen popped up with the title *Vine by Vine* by Rena Fairfield Montgomery.

Tony began reading the first chapter.

Roots.

In order to make great wine, you need good terroir, meaning the soil, climate and topography of a region that uniquely influence the grapes. A wine with a certain terroir cannot be reproduced in close resemblance of another, because the terroir is not exactly the same. Much like the DNA of a person each wine has a one-of-a-kind profile.

I guess I came from good terroir. That is to say, my parents were solid grounded people, rich, not by monetary standards but by life and vitality and a grand love of winemaking. My roots run deep and strong. I come from healthy stock. I've always been thankful for that. I've had the love of the best two people on earth. A child can't ask for more than that.

My parents, like the trellis system of a vine, show you the way yet cannot dictate the path you will ultimately choose. As I grew I felt their protection, but as I look back I also see the strength they instilled in me. After all, a new vine needs to weather a vicious storm now and again. It needs to withstand blasting winds, bending by its might but not breaking.

I remember a time when I was in grammar school...

Tony read the chapter, smiling often as Rena portrayed anecdotes from her childhood, relating them to the ever-growing vines, taking shape, readying for the fruit it would bear.

He skimmed the next few chapters until he came upon a chapter called "Crush and Maceration."

The crush in vintner's terminology is when the grapes are harvested, broken from the vine by gentle hands. The crush happens each year between August and October, depending on the kind of grapes that are growing in your vineyard. For me, the crush happened only once. It's that time in your life when you break off from the ones that graciously and lovingly nourished you to become your own person. I was sixteen when that happened. I grew from an adolescent girl to womanhood the autumn of my sophomore year. The day I met my first love, Rod Barrington.

I had a big crush on Rod from the moment I laid eyes on him. He was new to our school, but his family was well known in the area. Everyone knew of the wealthy Barringtons, they owned more property in our valley than anyone else.

While my friendship with Rod grew, I fell more and more in love with him. For a young girl, the pain of being his friend nearly brought me to my knees. I couldn't bear seeing him tease and joke with other girls, but I kept my innermost feelings hidden, hoping one day he'd realize that his good friend, Joanie Adams might just be the girl for him.

Tony read a few more passages, skimming the words on the page quickly, absorbing each instance that Rena relayed in the story, vaguely recalling the circumstances much like Rena had written. It was clearly obvious that though Rena had changed the names, Rena had written about his relationship with her, reminding him of the love they once shared. As he read on, the smile disappeared from his face, Rena's emotions so bold and honest on the page. He knew he'd hurt her but just how much he hadn't known until this very moment.

In winemaking once the grapes are gently crushed from the skins, seeds and stems, allowing the juices to flow, maceration occurs. The clear juice deepens in color the longer it's allowed to steep with its counterparts, being in direct contact with stems and seeds and skins. Time blends the wine and determines the hue and flavor, intensifying its effect.

And that's how I felt about Rod. The longer I was with him, the more direct contact I had with him, the more I loved him. He colored my every thought and desire. I knew I'd met the man of my dreams. We blended in every way.

Tony skimmed more pages, his stomach taut with regret and pain. He stopped when he came to a chapter titled "Corked."

He knew what that meant. He forced himself to read on.

Wine that is "corked" has been contaminated by its cork stopper, causing a distinctly unpleasant aroma. The wine is ruined for life. It's spoiled and will never be the same. Fortunately for wine lovers, only seven percent of all wine is considered corked or tainted. A sad fact if you'd invested time and energy with that bottle.

Wine shouldn't let you down. And neither should someone you love.

Tony ran his hands down his face, unable to read any more. But a voice inside told him he had to know the extent of Rena's feelings. He had to find out what happened to her after he'd left her. He continued to read, sitting stiffly in the chair, woodenly reading words that would haunt him.

"Rod called today, after his first big sale. It killed me to talk to him, I felt selfish for wishing he'd flop in his high-powered position in New York. I was dealing with my mother's terminal cancer, needing him so badly."

After reading Rena's story, which ended abruptly when Rena's mother died, Tony slumped in the seat.

Drained, hollowed out by what he'd learned, he simply sat there, reliving the scenarios in his mind.

Eventually Tony logged off of his computer, leaving the disk behind, but Rena's emotions and her silent suffering while he was winning races and pursuing his dreams would stay with him forever.

He met Joe at the office at six o'clock as planned, his disposition in the dumps. "Did you find anything unusual?" he asked his brother.

"No, not unusual. Dad did screw a lot of people over, but I've never seen it so clearly as now."

Tony groaned, his mood going from gray to black in a heartbeat. "I was hoping I was wrong."

"No, you're not wrong. Your instincts are dead-on." Joe shuffled papers around, comparing notes he'd written.

"Looked to me like Dad deliberately undersold cabernet and merlot to the retailers to drive Purple Fields out of business. We make five kinds of wine, but he chose the two Purple Fields are famous for to undercut them. From what I've found, he sold for a slight loss for at least ten years. He knew he could sustain those losses without a problem, while Purple Fields couldn't compete."

Tony winced, hearing the truth aloud. "I'd asked Dad to leave Purple Fields alone. To let them make a living. But I'm betting he did it to spite me."

Joe's brows rose. "You think he singled them out because you chose a different career?"

"He'd never approved of my choices. He didn't want me to succeed. He wanted to dictate the course of my life, and it pissed him off that I wouldn't listen to him. I chose racing over him."

"Yeah, Dad was angry when you took off. He wanted to hand down his business to his firstborn son. Hell, he wasn't too fond of me not sticking around either. I've got a head for business, not grape growing."

Tony's lips curved halfway up. "You're a computer geek, Joe."

"And proud of it," Joe added, then focused his attention back on the subject at hand. "Dad was an all-around brute. I bet he used the same tactics on half a dozen other small wineries to drive them out of business."

"Doesn't make it right. Hell, he made millions. He didn't need to shut down his competition."

"Apparently, he didn't see it that way."

Tony let go a frustrated sigh. "At least there's something I can do about it. I'm going to renegotiate those contracts. We'll sell our wine at a fair price, but we won't undercut anyone, especially Purple Fields."

Joe nodded and leaned back in his chair. "That should make Rena happy."

"Yeah, but it won't make up for all the past pain this family put her through."

"You're not just talking about Dad now, are you?"

Tony took a steadying breath and shook his head. "No. But I plan to make it up to Rena. Whether she likes it or not."

"Those sound like fighting words, Tone."

Tony rose from his seat. "They are."

"Oh, before I forget, someone called for you today."

Joe shifted through a pile of notes, coming up with one. "Something about your racing contracts. They've been calling the house and couldn't reach you."

He handed Tony the note, and when he glanced at the name, he cursed under his breath. He didn't need this right now. "Okay," he said, stuffing the note in his pocket. "Thanks. I'll take care of it."

Now he had three things to deal with, the note he tucked away being the least of his worries. At least he knew now how to save Purple Fields, but after reading *Vine by Vine,* Tony wasn't sure how he could repair the damage he'd done to Rena.

The promise he made to David far from his mind, Tony wanted to save his hasty marriage for more selfish reasons. He couldn't deny that reliving the past in these last few hours made him realize how much Rena had once meant to him.

He got in his car and drove off, speeding out of town, needing the rush of adrenaline to ward off his emotions and plaguing thoughts that he was falling in love with Rena again.

Tony entered the house, and a pleasing aroma led him straight to the kitchen. He found Rena standing at the stove top stirring the meal, her hair beautifully messy and her face pink from puffs of steam rising up. She didn't acknowledge his presence initially until he wrapped his arms around her waist and drew her against him. He kissed her throat, breathing in her citrus scent. "Looking good."

"It's just stew."

"I meant you," Tony said, stealing another quick kiss. Coming home to this domestic scene, something grabbed his insides and twisted when he saw her. "You're beautiful behind the stove. I want to come home to you every night."

She frowned and moved slightly away. "Don't say those things."

"Why?" he asked softly. "Because I've said them before and now you don't believe me?"

Rena kept stirring the stew. "You're astute."

"And you're being stubborn."

She shrugged, moving away from the stove to grab two plates from the cabinet. Tony took out cutlery from a drawer and set two glasses on the table.

So now they were resorting to name-calling? This certainly wasn't the scene Tony pictured in his mind when he first entered the house.

"Did you find out anything from Joe?" Rena asked.

"Yeah, I did. But let's eat first."

"Whenever someone says that to me, I know the news is not good."

"There's bad news and there's good news. I think we should eat first before discussing it."

Rena brought the dishes to the stove top and filled their plates, adding two biscuits to Tony's plate. She served him and sat down to eat. Her long hair fell forward as she nibbled on her food. She wore jeans and a soft baby-blue knit blouse that brought out the vivid color of her eyes. She hardly looked pregnant, except for a hint of added roundness to her belly.

Sweeping emotions stirred in his gut. He wanted to protect Rena. He wanted to possess her. He wanted to make love to her until all the pain and anger disappeared from her life. So much had happened to her in her short thirty-one years from losing her mother and father, to losing David, but it had all started with him. And Tony determined it would all end with him as well.

After the meal, Rena started cleaning up. Tony rose and then took her hand. "Leave this. We'll take care of it later. We need to talk."

She nodded and followed him into the living room. Oak beams, a stone fireplace stacked with logs and two comfortable sofas lent to the warmth of the room. Tony waited for her to sit, then took a place next to her.

They sat in silence for a minute, then Tony began. "What I have to say isn't easy. Joe and I went through the records and have proof now of how my father manipulated sales in the region."

"You mean, my father was right? Santo set out to destroy us?"

Tony winced and drew a breath. "I can't sugarcoat it, Rena. My father undercut Purple Fields, even at a loss to his own company to drive you out of business. Joe's guess is that it wasn't personal. He'd been doing the same to other small businesses for years."

Rena closed her eyes, absorbing the information. "My father knew. He didn't have proof. His customers wouldn't talk about it, except to say that they'd found better deals elsewhere. They'd praised our wine over and over but wouldn't buy it."

"My father probably strong-armed them into silence," Tony said.

Rena opened her eyes and stared at him. He couldn't tell what was going on in her head, but he suspected it wasn't good.

She rose from her seat and paced the floor. "My mother was worried and anxious all the time. She loved Purple Fields. She and my father poured everything they had into the winery. They worked hard to make ends meet. She held most of it in, putting up a brave front, but I could tell she wasn't the same. My father noticed it, too. He'd stare at her with concern in his eyes. And that all started around the time when we broke up and you left town."

Tony stood to face her. He owed Rena the full truth or at least the truth as he saw it. His voice broke when he made the confession, "I think he targeted Purple Fields after I left."

She stiffened and her mouth twisted. "My God," she whispered, closing her eyes in agony. "Don't you see? The stress might have triggered my mother's illness."

Tony approached her. "Rena, no."

She began nodding her head. "Oh, yes. Yes. My mother was healthy. There was no history of that disease in our family. Mom was fine. Fine, until the winery started going downhill. She worried herself sick. The doctors even suggested that stress could be a factor."

Rena's face reddened as her pain turned to anger. She announced with a rasp in her voice, "I need some air."

Tony watched her walk out of the house, slamming

the door behind her. He ran a hand through his hair, his frustration rising. "Damn it. Damn it."

He'd never hated being a Carlino more than now. He could see it in Rena's eyes—the blame, the hatred and the injury. When she'd looked at him that way, he understood all of her resentment. He knew she'd react to the truth with some degree of anger, but he'd never considered that she'd blame his family for her mother's illness.

Could it be true?

Tony couldn't change the past. All he could do now was to convince her he'd make things right. He gave her a few minutes of solitude before exiting the house. He had to find his wife and comfort her.

Even though in her eyes, he was the enemy.

Nine

Rena ran into the fields. The setting sun cast golden hues onto the vines, helping to light her way. She ran until her heart raced too fast and her breaths surged too heavy. Yet she couldn't outrace the burning ache in her belly or the plaguing thoughts in her mind. She stopped abruptly in the middle of the cabernet vines, fully winded, unable to run another step. Putting her head in her hands, tears spilled down her cheeks. Grief struck her anew. It was as if she was losing her mother all over again. Pretty, vivacious Belinda Fairfield had died before her time. Her sweet, brave mother hadn't deserved to suffer so. She hadn't deserved to relinquish her life in small increments until she was too weak to get out of bed.

Rena's sobs were absorbed in the vines, her cries

swallowed up by the solitude surrounding her. Her body shook, the release of anguish exhausting her.

Two strong arms wrapped around her, supporting her sagging body. "Shh, Rena," Tony said gently. "Don't cry, sweetheart. Let me make it right. I'll make it all right."

"You…can't," she whispered between sobs. Yet Tony's strength gave her immeasurable comfort.

"I can. I will. We'll do it together."

Before Rena could formulate a response, Tony lifted her up, one arm bracing her legs and the other supporting her shoulders. "Hold on to me," he said softly, "and try to calm down."

Rena circled one arm around his neck and closed her eyes, stifling her sobs, every ounce of her strength spent.

Tony walked through the vineyard, holding her carefully. In the still of the night all that she heard was the occasional crunch of shriveled leaves under Tony's feet as he moved along.

When he pushed through the door to her house, her eyes snapped open. He strode with purpose to the bedroom and lay her down with care, then came down next to her, cradling her into his arms once again. "I'm going to stay with you until you fall asleep."

Rena stared into his eyes and whispered softly, "I hate you, Tony."

He brushed strands of hair from her forehead with tenderness then kissed her brow. "I know."

The sweetness of his kiss sliced through her, denting her well-honed defenses.

He took off her shoes and then his own. Next he undressed her, removing her knit top over her head and unzipping her jeans. She helped pull them off with a little tug, ready to give up her mind and body to sleep.

Tony covered them both with a quilted throw and tucked her in close. She reveled in his warmth and breathed in his musky scent despite herself. "Just for the record, sweetheart," he began, "I'm not here just because of the promise I made to David. It goes much deeper than that. And I think you know it."

Rena flinched inwardly, confusion marring her good judgment. She should pull away from Tony, refusing his warmth and comfort. She couldn't deal with his pronouncement. She couldn't wrap her mind around what he'd just implied. Yet at the same time, she needed his arms around her. She needed to be held and cradled and reassured.

Was she that weak?

Or just human?

"Good night, Rena." Tony kissed her lips lightly, putting finality to the night. "Sleep well."

Rena slept soundly for the better part of the night but roused at 3:00 a.m. to find Tony gone from bed. Curious, she slipped on her robe and padded down the hallway. She found him sprawled out on the living room sofa with his eyes closed. He made an enticing sight, his chest bare, his long lean, incredible body and handsome face more than any woman could ever hope to have in a mate.

Rena shivered from the coolness in the room. She

grabbed an afghan from the chair and gently covered Tony, making sure not to wake him. She lingered for just one moment then turned to leave.

"Don't go," he whispered.

Surprised, Rena spun around to meet Tony's penetrating gaze. "I thought you were asleep."

"I was—on and off." Tony sat up, planting his feet on the ground and leaning forward to spread his fingers through his hair.

"Sorry if I disturbed your sleep."

Tony chuckled without humor. "You did. You do."

Stunned by his blunt honesty, Rena blinked.

"Sleeping next to you isn't easy, Rena." Tony shook his head as if shaking out cobwebs. "Sorry, I wish I could be more honorable, but you're a handful of temptation."

Rena's mouth formed an "oh."

Tony stared at her. "You shouldn't find it shocking that I want to sleep with you. You remember how we were together."

Rena's spine stiffened. "Maybe you should sleep in another room."

"I have a better idea." He took her wrist and tugged her down. She landed on his lap. Immediately, he stretched out on the sofa, taking her with him. "Maybe I should make love to my wife."

A gasp escaped from her due to his sudden move. "Oh."

He untied the belt on her robe, his tone dead serious. "I want you."

His hands came up to push the robe off her shoulders,

revealing the bra and panties she'd slept in. His appreciative gaze heated the blood in her veins. "You can't blame me for that."

"No. But for so many other things," she said quietly.

"I get it, sweetheart. I understand." Tony pulled the robe free, exposing her fully.

Positioned provocatively, feeling his hard length pressing against her, excitement zipped through her system. Her breathing rough, she barely managed to utter the question. "Do you?"

"Yes, I do. And I want to make it up to you. Let me do that," Tony said, cupping his hand around her head and bringing her mouth to his. He kissed her softly. "Let me wipe away the pain." Again his lips met hers. "Let me help you heal, sweet Rena. You've been through so much."

His sincerity, his tone, the breathtaking way he looked at her softened the hardness around her heart. She wanted to heal, to release her defenses, to feel whole again.

"Tony," she breathed out, unsure of her next move.

"It's your call, sweetheart," he said, stroking her back in a loving way that created tingles along her spine. Another notch of her defenses fell.

Images flashed of the good times she'd had with Tony. The fun, the laughter and the earth-shattering lovemaking they'd shared. As much as she wanted to forget, the good memories came back every time he touched her. "I want the pain to go away," she whispered with honesty. Even if it was only for a short time tonight.

"Then let me take you there."

She closed her eyes, nodding in relief, surrendering herself to the moment. "Yes."

Rena touched his chest, her fingers probing, searching, tantalizing and teasing. He felt incredibly good. Strong. Powerful. She itched to touch him all over.

Bringing her head down to his, she claimed his mouth in a lingering kiss. She took it slow, pushing aside her misgivings. His body seemed in tune with hers. Every little action she took brought his sexy reaction. Every moan she uttered, he answered with a groan. She liked being in control. It was the first time she'd ever taken the reins so fully, and Tony seemed to understand what she needed. He encouraged her with a gleam in his eyes and a willing body.

"I'm all yours," he whispered.

Her breath caught. She knew he meant it sexually, but Rena seized on the reality of that statement. He was all hers. But what she didn't know was, could she ever be *all his?*

"You're thinking again," Tony scolded with a smile.

"Guilty as charged." Rena reached around to unhook her bra, freeing her breasts. Letting her bra drop, she freed her mind as well, pushing all thoughts away but the immediate here and now.

Tony reached for her then, his touch an exquisite caress of tenderness and caring. He kissed her lovingly, cherishing every morsel of her body with his lips and hands until his unexpected compassion seeped into her soul.

Their lovemaking was sedate and measured, careful and unflappable one moment, then crazy and wild, fierce and fiery the next. They moved in ups and downs, from highs to lows, they learned and taught, giving joy and pleasure to one another. The night knew no bounds. And when it came time to release their pent-up tension, Rena rose above Tony, straddling his legs. He held on to her hips and guided her. Taking him in felt natural, familiar and so right. She enjoyed every ounce of pleasure derived from their joining. She moved with restless yearning, her body flaming, all rational thought discarded.

Tony watched her, his eyes never wavering, his body meeting her every demand. He was the man she'd always wanted, the man she'd been destined to love. He'd pushed his way back into her life, but Rena couldn't trust in him, not fully, not yet. But each time they came together, her resolve slipped just a little, and her heartache slowly ebbed.

When she couldn't hold on any longer, her skin prickling, her flesh tingling and her body at its absolute limit, she moaned in ecstasy.

"Let go, sweetheart," Tony encouraged.

And she shuddered, her orgasm strong. She cried out his name when her final release came. Tony tightened his hold on her and joined her in a climax, taking them both to heaven.

Rena lowered down, spent. Tony wrapped her into his arms and kissed her forehead. "Do you still hate me?" he asked.

"Yes," she replied without hesitation. "But not as much as before."

Tony squeezed her tighter and chuckled almost inaudibly. "Guess, I'm going to have to work on that."

During the next week, Tony left Rena during the day to work on saving her winery. He made calls out of his Napa office, meeting with customers personally to explain the new pricing structures. Tony liked winning but not at the expense of others trying to eke out a living. If there was a contract he could renegotiate, Tony was on top of it.

He made sure that their company held their own in the marketplace, but with Joe's help they'd come up with a pricing plan that would realize profits and still allow the smaller wineries to compete.

Unlike his father, Tony didn't need to crush his opponents. The company's profits would go up on certain types of wine while the other local wineries of comparable quality would also make a profit on their specialties. It was a win-win situation in his opinion.

Satisfied with what he'd accomplished today, he called it quits, gathering up the papers on his desk. He was anxious to get home to Rena. Little by little, she was coming around, softening to him, smiling more and looking less and less guilty about their circumstances.

As he got ready to leave, he pondered how at night he'd join her in bed, and more times than not, they'd make love. Slow and sweet one time then wild and hot another time. Tony never knew what the night would bring. Some nights, when both were exhausted, they'd just fall asleep in each other's arms.

Tony enjoyed waking up next to Rena in the mornings. With her hair messy and her eyes hazy with sleep, she'd look at him and smile softly for a second or two before her memories returned and a haunted look would enter her eyes.

He clung to those few seconds in his mind, telling himself that one day that troubled look would be gone forever and she'd accept him completely as her husband and the father of her baby.

Tony smiled at the thought. Rena's stomach showed signs of the baby now. He was amazed at how quickly her body had transformed, her belly growing rounder each day.

"Excuse me, Tony," Ali said, stepping into his office.

Tony glanced at her, and as usual, the same thought flitted in his mind. He couldn't believe Joe wasn't interested in this vital, gorgeous, very capable woman.

"There's a call for you. From your agent. A mister Ben Harper? He says it's important. Line one."

Tony's smile faded. "Okay, thanks." He glanced at the flashing red light. He couldn't ignore Harper anymore. "I'll get it in here."

He waited until Ali walked away before picking up the phone. "Hello, Ben."

His agent read him the riot act for not returning his calls. Tony slammed his eyes shut, listening to his tirade.

"You know damn well you're under contract. My ass is on the line, too."

"It's not a good time right now," Tony said.

"You told me that two months ago. They gave you an extension because of your father's death, and you were recovering from your injuries, but I can't put them off much longer. They're threatening a lawsuit, for heaven's sake. You need to give me something. *Now,* Tony."

Tony sighed into the receiver, caving in to these last few contractual commitments. He still had an endorsement deal with EverStrong Tires and was expected to do interviews for a few of the races. "How long will it take?"

"Filming could take up to a week for the commercial."

"When?"

"Yesterday."

"Make it for next week, Ben. I'll do my best."

"You better be there, Tony. You've pushed them too far as it is. And don't forget, you're expected at Dover International Speedway for the first interview."

"I'll be there."

"I'll call you with the details."

"I'm holding my breath," he mumbled and hung up. He paced the office, shaking his head. Things were just getting better with Rena, and he didn't want that to end.

Rena hated anything to do with racing. Understandably so, but Tony had no choice in the matter. The last thing he needed was a lawsuit. And, if he were truly honest with himself, he missed the racing scene. Tony had recognized that it was time to leave it behind. Exit while still on top, they say. He'd accomplished what he'd set out to do, but a man doesn't lose his passion that easily. His blood still stirred with excitement when he stepped foot on the raceway.

The difference was that now Rena and the baby took precedence over racing. He was committed to his marriage and determined to get that same commitment from her.

Tony left the office and drove to Purple Fields, eager to see Rena. He entered the house and found her finishing a conversation on the phone in the kitchen. He came up behind her and wrapped his arms around her waist, his hands spreading across her stomach. He caressed her tiny round belly and nibbled on her throat. It had only been a few days that she'd allowed him this intimacy, and Tony couldn't get enough. "Who was that?" he asked, setting his chin on her shoulder.

"The doctor's office. I have an appointment tomorrow."

"What time are we going?"

"We?" Rena turned in his arms. "You can't go with me, Tony."

He blinked. "Why not?"

Rena stared at him. "You know why."

Tony's brows furrowed. "No, I don't. You tell me."

She moved out of his arms and shrugged. "This is David's baby."

Tony rolled his eyes. "I'm aware of that." She reminded him every chance she could. "So?"

"No one knows we're married. How would it look if I showed up with you?"

Tony summoned his patience and spoke slowly. "It would look like a good friend is supporting you at your doctor's appointment."

"No," she said adamantly. "I can't. Solena is taking me."

"No, *I'm* taking you."

Rena's eyes closed as if the prospect disturbed her sanity. Tony's ire rose, and he calmed down by taking a few breaths. "Maybe it's time to expose our marriage. Then you'd have a legitimate reason to have me there."

She shook her head. "I'm not ready for that."

"Why, Rena? Why not stop this ruse? We're living together. *We're married.* Don't worry about what people think. It's no one's business. This is about us, our lives and our family."

"It's not that," she rushed out, giving him her uplifted chin.

Tony stared at her. Then it dawned on him. "Oh, I see. You're not ready to accept me as your husband. As long as no one knows, you can pretend it isn't so. You can stay in your own world and not face reality."

Rena didn't deny it. She put her head down, refusing to let him see the truth in her eyes.

"Tell Solena I'm taking you tomorrow. I promised David and I won't break that promise."

But Tony's truth was that he wanted to be beside Rena during her appointment. He wanted to provide for her and protect her. He wanted to lend her support. And more and more, he found his desire had nothing to do with the vow he made to his best friend.

"Everything looks great, Rena. You're in good health. The baby has a strong heartbeat," Dr, Westerville said, smiling her way.

"Thank you, Doctor." Sitting upright in a green-and-white checkered gown on the exam table, Rena sighed in relief. Though she felt fine, hearing it from the doctor relieved her mind.

After he'd finished the checkup he'd reminded her of the do's and don't's regarding her pregnancy. Eat smaller meals, more times a day. Keep on a healthy diet. Stay active, but don't overdo anything.

Rena had been doing all those things since even before her first appointment with the doctor. The second she realized she was having a baby, she'd read everything she could about pregnancy and gestation.

"I'll let your friend in now," the doctor said.

She gave him a small smile.

The doctor opened the exam room door and let Tony inside. She'd relented in letting him take her to the appointment, but absolutely refused to have him in the room during the examination.

Tony walked a few steps into the room with his concerned gaze pinned on her. Before she made introductions, she answered his silent questions. "I'm fine and the baby is healthy. Dr. Westerville, this is David's good friend, Tony Carlino."

"Of course." The doctor put out his hand. "Nice

to meet you Mr. Carlino. I've been a fan of yours for years."

Tony nodded and shook the doctor's hand. "I appreciate that."

"All of us locals have rooted for you since day one."

Tony accepted his compliment with grace. "I've had a lot of support from this area. It means a lot. But now I'm retired and home to stay." He turned to Rena and she shot him a warning look. "Rena's a family friend. I plan to help her as much as possible."

"That's good. She's doing fine. She's very healthy and I don't foresee any problems. With all you've been through these past few months," the doctor said, focusing back on her, "it's very good to have a friend go through this with you. I recommend childbirth classes in a month or two, but for now, just follow the list of instructions I gave you."

"I'll do my best."

"Still running the winery?" he asked.

She nodded. "I promised David I'd keep Purple Fields going. Not that I want anything different myself."

"Okay, good. But in your later months, you may have to back off a little. Delegate duties more and—"

"I'll see to it," Tony chimed in. "I'll make sure she takes it easy."

The doctor glanced at Tony, then at Rena. He smiled warmly. Heat crawled up her neck, and at the same time, she wanted to sock Tony into the next county.

Dr. Westerville patted her shoulder. "I'll see you next month, Rena. I know your husband would be proud of

you and glad you're going to have the support you need."
He turned and shook Tony's hand once again. "David
was a good man and it seems that he picked his friends
wisely."

When he left the room, Rena glared at Tony. "I need
to get dressed."

"I'll help." He grinned.

She shot him another warning look.

"Come on, Rena. Lighten up. The baby is healthy
and so are you. That's good news."

Rena sighed and admitted joy at her baby news, but
it struck her anew that she'd be going through all of this
with Tony. "Can't you see that this is hard for me?"

"I know, Rena. You remind me every half an hour."

Rena twisted her lips. "No, I don't."

"Seems like it," Tony muttered. "I'll wait for you
outside."

She stepped down from the table and walked into the
small dressing area, untying her gown and throwing on
her clothes. Had she been too hard on Tony? At times,
she felt like a shrew, but it was only because every
time she softened to him, she felt like she was losing
another piece of David. Little by little, David's memory
was fading. And that wasn't fair to him or to her. A
woman needed time to grieve and recover. But Tony
had bounded into her life, hell-bent on keeping the vow
he'd made to David.

Her feelings were jumbled up inside and half the time
she didn't know which emotions were honest and true.
She'd never been in a situation remotely like this. She

chuckled at the absurdity—she was a secretly married, pregnant widow.

Not too many women could say that.

After Rena's doctor's appointment, Tony took her to lunch at her favorite little café in town. Thinking about the new life growing inside her, she couldn't deny her happiness. Seeing Dr. Westerville made it all seem real, and knowing that the baby was healthy and hearing the due date for the birth lightened her heart. The joy and love she held inside couldn't be duplicated.

After they ate their meal, they stopped at an electronics store where she and Tony ordered a top-of-the-line computer with all the bells and whistles. To overcome her resistance to such a complex-looking computer, Tony had promised to set it up when it arrived and get her acquainted with it. Whatever they couldn't figure out, his brother Joe would certainly be glad to explain to them.

Tony made other purchases as well—new phones for the house and office and a four-in-one fax machine he insisted they needed at Purple Fields. She certainly couldn't fault her husband his generosity. Where she and David had pinched pennies to make a go of the winery, Tony had no trouble spending money for the cause. Of course, he was a millionaire in his own right, famous in the world of racing, and he could afford these things.

They strolled down the street past a baby store, the window displaying a white crib and matching tallboy dresser, strollers and car seats. Rena lingered for a moment, aching with yearning.

"Rena, any time you're ready," Tony said.

Her emotions kept her from taking the next step. Something held her back. "Maybe soon. First I have to clean out the room and paint it. I thought we'd use the room across from ours to be closer to the baby."

Tony surprised her with a kiss. "It's a great idea."

Her gaze lifted to his noting the pleased gleam in his eyes. She'd *surprised* both of them with her comment, but more and more she was learning how to trust him again. So far, he hadn't given her any reason not to. He'd made good on his promise to fix Purple Fields. He'd spoken with customers and renegotiated contracts all in order to save her from ruin. He'd been patient with her. He'd been kind. He'd been a magnificent lover and a good friend.

He'd set out to prove that he wasn't like his ruthless father, and so far, he'd succeeded. If she could put the past behind her, they stood a chance. For her baby's sake, if not her own, she wanted to take that chance.

"I'll help you with the room. I'm pretty good with a paintbrush. What color?"

Rena grinned, letting go a little bit more of the pain trapped inside. "Sage-green or chiffon-yellow."

"What, not pink or blue?"

Rena tilted her head and sighed. "We don't know the baby's sex yet." She glanced inside the store again, then placed her hand over her belly and admitted, "I don't want to wait until we find out."

"Me, either," Tony said, taking her hand. "Let's go find us some sage and chiffon paint. There's a hardware store up ahead."

By the time they returned home, Rena was in the best mood she could remember. They'd picked out paint colors together—unable to decide, they'd bought gallons of each shade—paintbrushes, rollers and drop cloths.

"Do you really want to help me paint the bedroom?" Rena asked after dinner as they retired to the living room. The day had exhausted her physically. Tony sat beside her on the sofa, and he brought her into the circle of his arms. She rested her head on his chest.

"You doubt me after I badgered that salesman with questions about baby-safe paint for half an hour?"

A wave of excitement stirred as she envisioned her baby's room all fresh and clean, filled with furniture, just waiting for his or her arrival. And Tony had been there every step of the way. She'd resisted giving him anything more than her body, but Tony wasn't a man she could easily put out of her mind. Ever so slowly he was making inroads to her heart. "I'm anxious to start."

"I'll clear my calendar, and we can start tomorrow," Tony said. "We'll have it done by the weekend."

"Oh, I can't. I have a vendor coming for an appointment tomorrow. We have three wine tours booked this week, and I can't leave Solena to do it all. Can we start on it first thing next week? Monday?"

Tony looked into her eyes, hesitating. Then he rose to stand before the large double window facing the front yard, his hands on his hips. "I can't do it next week, Rena."

His tone alarmed her. "Why not?"

He scrubbed his jaw a few times, as if searching for the right words. "I was going to tell you tomorrow." He paced the room, walking slowly as he spoke. "I'm up against a wall. I have commitments I made a long time ago, and my agent can't find any wiggle room. I'm going out of town on Sunday. I'll be gone at least a week."

"A week?" Rena's heart plummeted. A serious case of déjà vu set in.

I won't be gone long, Rena. I'll come back as soon as I can. Or you can come meet me. We'll be together somehow, I promise.

"What are you going to do?" she asked.

"Some interviews and a commercial. It's one of the last endorsements I'm contracted to do."

Rena felt numb. "Okay," she said once she'd gathered her wits. She kept her voice light, her tone noncommittal. "You don't need my permission." She rose from the sofa. "I have some work to do to prepare for my meeting tomorrow."

"I'll help you," Tony said, gauging her reaction.

Rena could only manage a curt reply. "No. I can do it myself."

Tony approached her. "Rena?"

She halted him with a widespread hand. "It's okay, Tony. Really. I understand."

"Damn it! You don't understand." Frustration carried in his deep voice. His olive complexion colored with heat. "I've put this off for as long as I can. They'll sue me if I don't show up, and that's not what either of us needs right now."

"You don't have to explain to me." She hoisted her chin and straightened her shoulders. "I never wanted any of this to begin with."

Tony strode to face her. Taking her into his arms, he yanked her close and narrowed his eyes. "This isn't twelve years ago. The situation is different. You think I won't come back?"

"Darn right, it's different. I'm not that love-smitten young girl anymore. Whether you come back or not, I know I'll survive. I did it once and I can do it again."

Tony released her arms and then barked off a dozen curses, each one fouler than the next.

"As far as I'm concerned, you owned up to your obligation to David. You married me. Purple Fields is on its way to becoming solvent again. I won't fool myself into thinking we have anything more. You did your duty, Tony. Congratulations."

"Anything else?" Tony asked, clearly fuming.

"Yes," she said, unmindful of his state of anger. She was plenty angry, too. To think he'd nearly had her fooled that they might have something to build on. But somehow, racing had always come between them. David was gone to her. But Tony? She'd never really had him to begin with, and this was a brutal reminder that she would always come in second place. "Thanks for ruining the best day I've had since my husband died."

Ten

Nick and Joe were relaxing outside on the patio overlooking the Carlino vineyards when Tony strode in. The stone fire pit provided light and heat on this cool spring night. The weather was always cooler atop their hillside than in the valley below, and tonight, Tony welcomed the brisk air.

His brothers welcomed him with curious stares. "Want a beer?" Nick asked.

Tony shook his head. "I need a real drink." He strode over to the outside bar and poured himself two fingers of whiskey. Without pause, he gulped down one finger's worth of the golden liquid before returning to sit on a patio chair facing the flames. He slouched in his seat, stretched out his long legs and crossed one ankle over the other, deep in thought.

After several moments of awkward silence, Nick asked, "What's up, Tony?"

Tony sipped his whiskey. "What? Can't a guy come home to spend some time with his brothers?"

Joe and Nick chuckled at the same time.

"Seriously, why are you here?" Joe asked.

The fire crackled, and Tony watched the low-lying flames dance. "I had to tell Rena I still have racing obligations. I'm leaving on Sunday for a week. She didn't take the news well."

"She's mad?" Nick asked.

Tony shook his head. "Worse. She's indifferent. She's not sure I'll come back and pretty much told me she doesn't care."

"She's recalling past history, Tone. She's protecting herself," Joe said.

"I know. But the hell of it is that we were working out our problems, getting closer, until this came up. What am I supposed to do? My agent's butt is on the line. Ben's been with me since the beginning, and he's been a loyal friend. I owe him. If I get sued for breach of contract, it reflects on him, too."

"It's not like you can tell anyone you have a pregnant wife at home," Nick added. "Ben doesn't know?"

"No, he doesn't. There's no need to tell him." Tony finished his whiskey, not revealing his opinion about the subject. He'd tell the world about their marriage, if Rena would agree. "The problem is that we were getting closer. I took her to the doctor today. We'd planned on fixing up the nursery together. It's the first time she's let me in. And it felt good. Damn good. If I had any choice at all, I'd stay here and paint the baby's room instead of flying off to do a commercial."

"Wow," Nick said, catching his gaze. "I didn't realize you were in love with Rena."

Tony couldn't deny it. He set his glass down and stared into the flames. "I don't think I ever stopped loving her."

"You two are a perfectly matched set," Nick offered, his statement hitting home.

Joe sighed. "I'm the last one to give advice on romance, Tony. But it seems to me from a logical standpoint that you need a gesture of some sort. Some way to show her how much she means to you."

"You mean like blowing off this deal?"

"No, by asking her to go with you."

"She won't go. She hates anything to do with racing. It would just remind her of all the bad things that have happened in her life."

"Then I suppose you'll just have to make it up to her when you get back."

Tony agreed. He'd have a lot of making up to do. "Listen, will you two check on her next week while I'm gone?"

"Sure." Joe nodded.

Nick added, "No problem. I like Rena. She's family now, and I don't have much on my nightly agenda at the moment."

"Which means you're not dating three women at the same time," Joe said, with a teasing grin.

"Never three." Nick leaned back in his chair and

sipped his beer. Thoughtful, he added, "I only date one lady at a time. I like to keep things simple."

"You're not off to Monte Carlo anytime soon, then?" Tony asked.

"No. I'm here for a while. The contractors have the renovations at my house under control and it'll be ready soon enough. At least dad's timing was good in that respect."

Tony exchanged a glance at Joe. Of the three, Nick held the deepest grudge against Santo Carlino. With good reason, but the damage was done and they all had to move on with their lives.

"Besides," Nick added, "I told you I'd help out with the company for as long as it takes. Once we figure out which of you two will be running the company, I'm moving back there."

"What makes you think it'll be me or Tony?" Joe asked.

"Because it sure as hell won't be me. You know how I feel about this place."

Tony raised his brows. "It's just us now, Nick. Santo is gone."

Nick ignored him. "You're both invited. You've never seen my place in Monte Carlo. I want you to come as soon as you can."

Tony rose from his seat, ready to get back home to Rena. Talking with his brothers had helped. He'd gotten his dilemma off his chest, but he wasn't at all sure that they'd come up with a solution. "I'll feel better leaving knowing you both will call Rena and stop by Purple Fields for a visit."

"We have your back," Joe said.

"Thanks. I appreciate it."

"You leaving already?" Nick asked.

"Yep, I'm going home to my wife." He needed to see her. He had to sort out their differences and try to make his marriage work.

Rena's last parting comment had stung him.

Thanks for ruining the best day I've had since my husband died.

He was her husband now.

It was time Rena realized that.

The next three nights Rena claimed exhaustion, turning in early and falling asleep long before Tony came to bed. In the morning, she'd find herself tangled up in his arms. He hadn't pressed her for more. In fact, she admired the patience and consideration he'd shown her. He'd kiss her hello in the morning, then rise from bed early.

They lived life like a married couple. He'd shave in front of her, and she'd catch glimpses of him showering, the vision often lingering in her mind long after he'd toweled off and dressed. She cooked for him and cleaned his clothes, and he thanked her politely.

Often, he'd take a cup of coffee and buttered toast into the office and not come out until well past noon. He spent a great deal of time working on her books, but once in a while she'd spot him out in the vineyards speaking with Raymond or checking the vines.

She found him today amid the merlot grapes. "The

computer just arrived. And all the other things you ordered."

"Great," he said, squinting into the bright sunshine. "I'll be right there. With any luck, I'll get it up and running before I leave tomorrow."

"Okay," she said, not in any hurry to return to the office. Her mind was in a jumble. On the one hand, she didn't know if she could trust Tony's intentions, but on the other hand she hoped she wasn't making a big mistake by misjudging him.

She'd spoken with Solena about Tony leaving for a week to keep his contractual obligations. Rena had been honest about her feelings and concerns, and while Solena had always been supportive, this time she hadn't seen it Rena's way.

"Are you sure you're being fair to him?" she'd asked. "Doesn't seem like he has much choice in the matter. Or maybe there's more to your anger than that?"

"Like what?" Rena had asked.

Her friend had given her a knowing, yet sympathetic, look. "Like maybe you want to keep friction between the two of you because you're falling in love with him again."

Tony broke into her thoughts, staring at her over her obvious reluctance to leave. He cast her a big smile. "Is there anything else?"

Her heart lit up. "No, nothing else. I'll be giving a wine tour in a few minutes. I'd better go."

"Yeah, me too. I'll walk with you."

He put his hand to her lower back, and together they left the fields.

"Tony?" she began, as they headed for the house.

He looked up. "Hmm?"

She stopped at the very edge of the vineyard and peered into his eyes. Sunlight cast a glow over his dark hair and deepened his olive skin. He was gorgeous-times-ten, and that never hurt his cause. But she had loved the man *inside* that hunky body, the one who'd slay dragons for her. Or so she'd believed.

"I may have overreacted the other day."

His brows rose.

"I'm not saying I did, but just that there's the possibil—"

"Shut up, Rena." The softness of his tone belied his harsh words.

He grabbed her waist and yanked her against him, taking her in a crushing, all-consuming kiss. When the kiss ended, she opened her eyes and swayed in his arms, feeling quite dizzy.

"How long before your tour group shows up?" he asked in a rasp, nuzzling her throat.

"Ten minutes."

Tony groaned. Then he kissed her once more, bringing her body up against his again, fitting them perfectly together. "Tonight, after dinner."

Rena's breath caught in her throat. She couldn't pretend she didn't know what he meant. She wouldn't protest. Sleeping next to him and waking up wrapped in his arms, pretending indifference hadn't been easy on her. She was a mass of contradictions when it came to Tony. But she wouldn't deny him. She wanted him. Not that her sexy husband would take no for an answer.

Judging by the hot gleam in his eyes or the way he'd just kissed her senseless, Rena knew they were in for a memorable night.

Dinner seemed to take forever. Rena fumbled with the meal, undercooking the potatoes and forgetting the garlic toast in the oven. They ate raw potatoes and burnt bread, and all the while Tony's gaze never wavered as he watched her stumble her way around the kitchen. She apologized a half dozen times, but Tony continued to eat her nearly inedible meal. "I'm not complaining, sweetheart."

Once they finished, he helped clear the dishes, moving about the kitchen and touching her whenever he could, a casual graze here, an accidental bump of the shoulders there. Rena's nerves stood on end. This was foreplay, Carlino style. And it was working! His dark, enticing eyes made her wish she was tumbling in the sheets with him rather than doing dishes by the sink.

Tony came up behind her, pressed his hips to her rear end and wrapped his arms around her, his hands just teasing the underside of her breasts. His warm breath teased her throat. If anyone could make her feel desirable wearing an old apron with her hands in soapy dishwater it was Tony.

"I know what I want for dessert," he whispered, nibbling on her neck.

The glass she'd been rinsing slipped from her hand and shattered in the sink. "Oh, no!"

Tony chuckled and turned her around to face him, his body pressed to hers. "Calm down, Rena. It's not as if you broke your parents' prized antique goblet. Like when you were a kid."

Rena's brows furrowed. "What?"

"You know, your great-grandmother's goblet that you broke when you were trying to surprise your mother by washing the whole set."

"I know what I did, Tony." Rena chewed on her lip, her mind reeling. She'd never told anyone about that incident. She'd replaced all the glasses in the curio praying her mother wouldn't notice that one of the eight were gone. "But how did you know? I never told a soul about that."

Tony blinked. A guilty expression crossed his features.

Rena shoved at his chest and moved away from him. Anger bubbled up. "You read my story, didn't you?"

Tony hesitated for a moment then nodded, not bothering to lie. "I did."

"How could you do that, Tony?" Rena's voice rose to a furious pitch. "That wasn't meant for anyone to read. I can't believe you'd invade my privacy like that!"

"Sorry, but I had to know."

"Know what?" she shouted. "That losing you had devastated my life? That when my mother was sick I cried for her every night, needing you so badly? That after she died, I was at my wit's end and David, poor David, came along and picked up my shattered life and made me whole again." Rena paced the kitchen floor, her temper flaring. "I needed to write that for myself, Tony. Don't you see? Those were my innermost, heartfelt thoughts. Those were mine and mine alone!"

Rena whipped her apron off and tossed it aside, her body trembling. Regret and remorse set in. "Damn it, Tony. You were never meant to read that."

"Maybe I needed to read it, Rena. Maybe it made me see what a big mistake I made back then."

"No," Rena said, shaking her head. She didn't want to hear any of this. Not now. It was far too late. "Save it, Tony. For someone who cares." She directed her gaze right at him. "I thought that maybe this marriage could work, but now I see it never will. You abused my trust one too many times. I want you to go, Tony."

Tony shook his head. "I'm not going anywhere."

"You did what you set out to do. You saved my winery. I'll make it on my own from here on out. I'm not afraid of hard work. You've repaid your debt to David."

"This isn't about David anymore, Rena. You know it and I know it."

Rena faced him dead-on, her bravado slowly dissipating. Tears threatened and she held them back yet her voice cracked with anguish. "I know nothing of the kind. Now I'm asking you to please leave my home. You were leaving me anyway tomorrow. What's one more night?"

"You're my wife, damn it. I'm not leaving you tonight."

"Fine, do whatever you want. That seems to be what you do best. Just leave me alone."

Rena walked out of the room with her head held high. She slammed the bedroom door and fell onto the bed, tears spilling down her cheeks.

Tony's vivid curses from the living room reached her

ears. She curled her pillow around her head, blocking the sound of her husband's frustrated tirade.

At least she knew that tomorrow morning he would be gone.

Eleven

Stubbornly, Tony refused to leave Rena's house. He'd made himself comfortable on the sofa, listening for her. Once he was sure she'd shed all of her tears and had fallen asleep, he opened the bedroom door to check on her.

She looked peaceful tucked in her bed, her face scrubbed of makeup, her thick, dark hair falling freely onto her pillow. She made an enticing picture, one gorgeous leg extending out of the tousled sheets, her body glistening in the slight moonlight streaming in.

Tony's heart lurched seeing her alone in that bed. Certainly the night hadn't ended on the happy note he'd planned. He wouldn't join her tonight. She'd made it clear what she thought of him. She'd made it even clearer that she didn't want him near her.

As complex as their situation was, Tony believed that they belonged together. He hoped that the time they'd spend away from each other would help her see that. He wouldn't even consider the possibility of not having Rena in his life.

Right now, she was angry with him. She had a temper. And so did he. They were both passionate people, and that's one of the things he loved most about Rena—her zest for life. She wasn't a wilting flower. Not by a long shot.

She'd been hurt many times by him and by his family, but she refused to let him make it up to her. It was as if she'd relished the rift they'd had so she wouldn't have to face facts. She wouldn't have to realize that she had strong feelings for him.

Tony closed the door quietly and took up a place on the sofa with a bottle of Purple Fields' award-winning merlot. He poured a glass and knew he wouldn't be sleeping any time soon. The wine would lull his senses somewhat, but Tony couldn't shake a bad feeling that had wedged its way into his gut.

Before sunrise, Tony rose from the sofa. He stretched out the kinks in his shoulders, slanting his head from side to side and shaking out the rest of his body. With stealth, he moved through the house to peek in on Rena again.

She slept.

Tony cast her one long look before turning back around. He showered in the bathroom down the hall, and once he was dressed in the same clothes he'd worn the night before, he made himself a cup of coffee and walked outside. Sipping the steamy brew, he glanced toward the winery, glad to see Raymond's car parked in front.

He found him checking on the crusher. "Morning," he said.

Raymond glanced at him. "It's a beautiful one."

Tony nodded, his mood not so bright. "Listen, I have a favor to ask. I have to go out of town for a while. Can I depend on you to check on Rena for me?"

"Sure, you can count on me. And Solena will be around all week, too. Those women are like two peas in a pod."

"Yeah, Solena's a good friend. Both of you are."

Raymond removed his latex gloves. "Is there any reason you're asking? Is Rena feeling poorly?"

"No, she's fine. It's just that," Tony began, scratching the back of his head, hating to admit this, "I doubt she'll take my calls when I'm gone. We had a disagreement, and she's being stubborn."

Raymond laughed. "I hear you. I'll keep an eye on her. You can call me anytime."

Relieved, Tony slapped him on the back. "Thanks. I appreciate it. Well, I'd better get going. I've got a plane to catch."

Tony drove to the Carlino estate and packed his clothes in a suitcase, hoping to find his brothers there. No one was around but the housekeeper and gardening crew. He'd been on his own, traveling from city to city for the better part of twelve years but had never felt the sense of desolation he felt now.

Tony knew it was a short trip and that he'd be back,

but leaving with Rena angry at him didn't sit right. He was sure no amount of persuading would change her mind. He conceded that they needed time away from each other, yet as his driver dropped him off at the airport and he boarded the plane heading for his first on-screen interview in Charlotte, North Carolina, as the retired champion, a sense of foreboding clutched him.

And as the plane landed and Tony was picked up by ESPN's limo driver, he couldn't shake the strange feeling in his gut.

Rena deliberately waited until she heard Tony's car pull away before she rose from bed and showered. Her anger had turned to sadness in the light of day, and her heart ached at the sense of loss she felt.

She'd tried trusting Tony, and he'd once again disappointed her. The situation was so darn tangled up in her mind, the past and present mingling into a giant miserable heartache. She had every reason to feel the way she did. Tony would always put *his* career and *his* life ahead of hers. He looked out for *numero uno*.

Even if she were able to put the past behind her, how could she trust him to raise her child? She couldn't bear the thought of him disappointing her child again and again. Scenarios played out in her head, and she envisioned Tony simply not being available when they needed him.

Rena dressed in a pair of stretch jeans that accommodated her growing belly and a loose tank top. She pulled her hair up in a ponytail and secured it with a rubberband.

She didn't have to give any wine tours today, which she deemed a good thing. Her heart just wasn't in it. She'd cried so hard last night that even now her breathing was less than even.

Digging deep in her soul, she'd have to admit that the house seemed empty without Tony here. He had a presence about him. Life wasn't dull when he was around. But Rena would have to get used to that. She'd be alone again. She'd come to the realization that maybe she wasn't meant to have anyone in her life.

She'd endured so many losses, and if it weren't for the new life she nurtured, she wouldn't know how to go on.

But the baby above all else gave her hope.

When a knock resounded at her door, her nerves jumped, and images of Tony returning home to her flashed instantly in her head.

She opened the door wide and faced Raymond. Disappointment registered, surprising her. She'd analyze that feeling later. "Oh, Ray. I didn't think you'd come to work today."

"I wanted to check in. Uh, I was checking the crusher and destemmer yesterday, and I didn't like the way they sounded."

"Is there a problem?"

"No, not really. They're just old. Don't work like they once did. I fiddled with the crusher a bit. We sure could use a new one."

"Well, maybe we'll be able to get one soon." Rena hoped so. They'd be making a profit again, thanks to

Tony. Purple Fields was due for some refurbishing. "There's a few things I'd like to change around here."

"Sure would be nice."

"Want to come in? I was just going to have some orange juice and toast. You're invited if you have time."

"No thanks, Rena. Solena fed me a big breakfast already." He patted his flat stomach.

She chuckled, shaking her head at the dark-haired man who'd become such a good friend. "I don't know where you put it." Raymond could eat like a truck driver, yet he remained lean and fit.

"One day it will catch up with me," he said, with a certain nod. "Well, I just wanted to say hello. Everything okay here?"

"Just fine. I plan to have a quiet day. Maybe do some reading."

"We're home today if you need anything."

"I won't. But thank you. I'll see you both tomorrow."

Rena bid farewell to Raymond and finished her breakfast. She sat down on her sofa and read five chapters of her book on what to expect as a new parent, did a load of laundry and as she walked down the hallway to put the folded linens away, she passed the empty nursery filled with paint cans. Excitement stirred in her stomach. Distraction kept her loneliness at bay, and she'd run out of things she'd wanted to do. Except for one.

"Why not?" she asked herself. "I have all the supplies I need."

You were going to paint the room with Tony.

"Can't wait around for something that might not happen," she grumbled, answering aloud her innermost thoughts.

Rena put on one of David's old shirts, grabbed a ladder from the supply room behind the winery and set out the drop cloths on the floor of her baby's room.

Sunshine beamed into the undressed windows, and warmth flowed into the room. She imagined a few months ahead, when her baby cooed with happiness in his crib, surrounded by all his things, the room a very light shade of sage-green.

"That's it," Rena said with a smile. "Not yellow, but green."

She grabbed her father's old boom box from the hall closet, dusted it off and plugged it in. She sang along with the pop music blaring from the radio, humming when she didn't know the words. She opened the paint can with a screwdriver and stirred the lead-free paint feeling assured that the fumes wouldn't hurt the baby.

When the phone rang, Rena turned the radio down and listened to the voice speaking into her answering machine.

"It's Tony. Just wanted you to know that I'm here in North Carolina. Rena, we need to talk when I get back. I know you won't believe me, but I miss you."

Rena squeezed her eyes shut. She nibbled on her lip, putting the paint roller down, wishing Tony wouldn't say those things. Though he sounded sincere, his words always contradicted his actions.

"Well, I guess you're not going to pick up the phone. I'll call you tomorrow. Goodbye, Rena."

Rena sunk down to the floor and sat there for a long time, rehashing everything in her mind. But the bottom line, whether she deemed it rational thinking or not, was that Tony had once again left her. He hadn't put her needs first.

Rena's mood shifted then. She'd been enjoying painting the baby's room until Tony ruined it—like he seemed to ruin everything else in her life. She had a good mind to tell him not to call again, but that would warrant her picking up the phone and speaking to him. She couldn't do that for fear of what she might say.

In truth, she didn't know how she'd react with him saying nice things to her from miles away.

She had no faith in him.

And yet she was deeply in love with him.

Yes, she finally admitted that she'd fallen in love with him when she'd been a lovestruck teen, and those feelings just wouldn't go away. Having him back in her life had rekindled that love, as much as she had fought it. As much as she didn't want it to be true. As much as she thought herself a fool for allowing him back into her heart.

"Why is it so complicated with you, Tony?" she whispered. "Why do you constantly torture me?"

On a deep sigh, Rena stood and decided to fight those feelings. She wouldn't allow Tony's phone call to mar the joy she'd felt just moments ago. She picked up the paint roller and continued on until she'd finished painting two walls. After an hour, she stopped and stepped back to view her work.

"Not bad," she said, her mood lightening. The sage paint on the wall dried to the prettiest hue of green.

She took a quick water break and peeled an orange she'd picked from her kitchen fruit basket. Sitting down at the table, she gobbled up orange wedges and rested for a while, flipping through a baby magazine, getting decorating ideas.

Eager to finish, she headed back into the nursery and turned the radio volume up. Frank Sinatra crooned, "Our Love Is Here to Stay," the disc jockey deeming the song ageless. Rena saw irony in the song's lyrics as she hummed the melody.

She positioned the ladder against the third wall where an opened window faced out toward acres of vineyards. Late afternoon air blew through the screen and cooled the room. "This is the best room for you," she said, laying a loving hand over her tiny round belly. It gladdened her heart that her child would see Purple Fields at its finest, when the leaves grew strong and tiny beads of grapes flourished to plumpness.

Rena filled the tray of paint atop the ladder and began rolling the uppermost part of the wall. When the news broadcast came on the radio, Rena tuned it out, too enthralled in baby thoughts to focus on anything the broadcaster had to say until she heard Tony's name mentioned. She stopped to listen.

"And in sports news, retired race car champion Tony Carlino is back on the scene. In an interview today in Charlotte, North Carolina, amid thousands of fans, Carlino admitted that he'd been contemplating a return to racing...."

The paint roller dropped from Rena's trembling hand. Sage-green paint splattered the walls in big drops as the roller hit the ground. Woozy, she swayed and grabbed for the top of the ladder, but her light-headedness won out. She lost her balance and fell backward, landing on the floor with a solid thud. Pain throbbed in her head just before the world went black.

Tony removed the microphone from his shirt the second the interview with the jackass newscaster was over, the whole time wishing he were back in Napa instead of sitting in a press booth in North Carolina, thousands of miles away from his wife. His mood had gone from resigned to irritated in two seconds flat, when the newscaster spun his words in a continual effort to press Tony about his nonexistent return to racing.

After a heated off-air exchange between them, Tony left the press box fed up with all the hoops he'd had to jump through today just to meet the terms of his contract.

He wasn't looking forward to spending the next few days making a commercial either. He didn't want to be here, not when he'd been making headway in his marriage to Rena. Day by day, in small increments, they were working through their problems. There seemed to be some light at the end of the tunnel. She'd started to trust in him again.

Now, she wouldn't return his calls.

And he couldn't blame her. He'd let her down, going back on promises he'd made to her.

His agent followed him outside the press booth

and they left the racing venue together. "Tony, what's eating you? I've never seen you react that way to an interviewer."

"You heard him, Ben. He wouldn't let up on me. How many times does he have to hear no?"

"You made your point." Ben, always the diplomat, tried to appease him, but Tony wasn't ready to let it drop.

"He misconstrued my words and circled around the truth. Make a note, I never want to do another interview with him." Hell, he didn't want to do another interview with *anyone*. It was becoming more and more clear where Tony's place was.

"Well, it's over and done with now. Forget about it." Ben slapped him on the back. "Come on, let me take you to dinner."

Tony shook his head. "No thanks. I'm beat. I'm going to head back to the hotel."

"Okay, get some rest. I'll see you in the morning for the commercial shoot."

Tony bid his agent farewell and took a limo back to his hotel. When he arrived at the Hyatt, instead of going to his room, he headed straight for the cocktail bar and ordered a double whiskey.

He sat there, thinking about his life and all he'd accomplished. He wasn't one to ever give up when he wanted something. He'd had obstacles in his way, but he'd never had much trouble overcoming them. At least, not until now, with Rena.

He felt a tap on his shoulder and turned to find a

beautiful young blond woman taking a seat beside him. "You're Tony Carlino, the racecar driver, aren't you?"

"That would be me." He sipped his drink.

"Would you like to buy me a drink?"

Tony stared at her and saw the bold, provocative look in her eyes. She made no bones about what she wanted; she had "groupie" written all over her meticulously salon-tanned body. At one time, he might have indulged her and welcomed the fringe benefits that would've come afterward. Now, his thoughts were of his pregnant wife and the miles between them.

He finished off his drink and set a fifty on the bar. "Sure, have whatever you want on me. I'm going home to my wife."

And hours later, Tony put the key in the lock and turned the doorknob to Rena's house. The three-hour time difference from the East Coast put him back in Napa in the late afternoon, and he was grateful for regaining those hours. He'd spent more time in the air today than he'd spent on the ground in North Carolina. Wondering about Rena's reaction when she saw him, Tony opened the door slowly.

"I'm the last one to give advice on romance, Tony. But it seems to me from a logical standpoint, you need a gesture of some sort. Some way to show her how much she means to you."

Joe's words had stayed with him, and grand gesture or not, Tony knew in his gut that he had to return home to Rena tonight—it had to be tonight.

There were things he had to say. He needed to

clear the air between them. Especially after what had happened in North Carolina earlier today.

"Rena?" he called out, noting how quiet the house seemed. Again, he called her name and was met with silence. He hadn't seen her in the fields when he'd driven up, but then he wasn't really on the lookout at that time. He strode down the hallway and heard static coming from a radio. "Rena, are you here?"

He followed the sound to the room across from their bedroom. One look inside made his skin crawl. "Oh my God." A pool of green paint oozed from an overturned paint tray, the drop cloth doing its best to contain the puddle. Near the radio on the floor, Tony spotted something red. Initially, he froze and prayed that it wasn't what he'd thought. He moved quickly and bent to touch the crimson liquid and bring it to his nose. It wasn't wine or paint.

It was blood.

"Rena's blood," he breathed out. Plaguing thoughts of her being injured and bloody raced through his mind. "No," he said, shaking his head. "Please, God."

His cell phone rang.

Tony answered it immediately. "Tony? It's Solena. I've got some news—"

"Where's Rena?" he bellowed into the phone.

"We just arrived at Napa Hospital. I'm in the ambulance. She took a fall—"

"I'm coming. I'll be there in ten minutes."

"Ten minutes? Where are you and how—"

"I'll explain later." Tony shut off the phone and ran out of the house. His main concern was to see Rena.

He climbed into his car and hit the road, driving twenty miles an hour above the speed limit. Luckily, the roads were nearly empty, but even if they hadn't been, it wouldn't deter him. Nothing was going to stop him from getting to Rena.

He arrived at the hospital in eight minutes and strode with purpose to the emergency room desk. The clerk questioned his relationship to Rena Montgomery. "Damn it, she's my wife." He clenched his fists.

"There's no paperwork to support that," the woman said, glancing once more at her files, then slanted a look at the security guard standing in the corner. Sometimes his fame made his life a living hell. Everyone thought they knew everything about him. "Her name is Rena *Carlino* now. We just got married."

The clerk blinked. "Oh, uh. Well, then Mr. Carlino, I'll let you right through."

She buzzed him in. "Third door to your left."

Tony was there in seconds. He found Rena on the hospital triage bed, her eyes closed, her head wrapped in a white bandage. Solena stood by her side and smiled when she saw him. "How did you get here so fast?" she whispered as she strolled over to him. She gave him a hug then guided him just outside the door. "We all thought you were in North Carolina."

Tony glanced back at Rena. It pained him to see her looking so frail and weak. "I was already home when you called. I found the room a wreck and panicked. What the heck happened?"

"I don't know, other than she fell off the ladder. I

stopped by with dinner for her. When she didn't answer the door, I got worried and used my key to get inside.

"Apparently, she hit her head on the radio when she fell. She was unconscious when I found her."

"How long ago?"

"You missed us by fifteen minutes."

Tony's heart ached. He was to blame for this. He knew it in his gut. "Has she woken up?"

"Yes, in the ambulance. We've been speaking on and off. She's a little woozy. The doctor wants her to rest while they are preparing for the CT scan."

"What did she say?"

"She was worried about the baby."

Tony closed his eyes and nodded. Immense fear coursed through his body and he sent up silent prayers. "Me, too."

That baby, that beautiful new life growing inside Rena was Tony's responsibility, too. But it was so much more. It was to be his first child. He already knew he loved that baby. Rena had been through too much pain in her life to endure another tragedy. Tony wouldn't allow it. As irrational as that sounded, he would make sure that Rena never knew another bad day.

"The doctor was optimistic. She has a concussion and a little bump on her head, but they don't think the fall affected the baby."

"That's good," Tony said with relief. He'd never forgive himself if something happened to the baby. Rena would be inconsolable, and he wouldn't blame her.

"I'm going in now. I'll stay with her," Tony said.

"Do you want me to stay, too?" Solena asked.

Tony shook his head. "No, I have to speak to her. There are things I really need to say."

Solena smiled. "I understand."

"It's a good thing you found her when you did. I can't thank you enough."

"You were only minutes behind," she said. Then she cast him a curious stare. "Why *are* you here? I thought you'd be gone a week or more?"

Tony drew oxygen into his lungs. "That's why I have to speak with Rena. I'm here, and I'm not leaving her again."

Rena lay with her eyes closed in the hospital bed feeling slight relief, the throbbing in her head much less painful now. She remembered the reason she was here. Solena had called for emergency help and had traveled with her in the ambulance. The events of the past day came to mind at a snail's pace—but with surprising clarity.

A gentle touch to her hand brought her eyes open. She knew that touch. It was the person she'd dreamed about. The one person she'd wanted to have by her side.

"Hi, sweetheart," Tony said. "You're going to be okay."

"Am I?" she whispered on a breath.

Tony nodded, his dark eyes soft and glistening. Had he teared up? "Your CT scan is perfect. Dr. Westerville said the baby is fine. You can go home later this morning if you feel up to it."

With a slight nod of her head, she choked out, "That's good news. I'm so relieved about the baby. If something happened…" She couldn't even manage the words. She couldn't go there, couldn't think of the possibility of another loss in her life. This one would crush her.

Tony took her hand and squeezed. "It didn't, honey. You both are going to be fine."

Rena sat up a little straighter in the bed, grateful the movement didn't cause her pain. "What time is it?"

"Five o'clock in the morning."

"Have you been here all night?"

"Right here," he assured her. "All night."

"But how? You were in North Carolina last I remember."

"Yeah, well. I shouldn't have gone in the first place. The minute I landed there I knew I'd made a mistake. I knew where my place was. And that place was with you."

"Tony?" Rena couldn't believe her ears. "What do you mean?"

"I did that interview, the whole time wishing I was with you."

Rena looked away then, unable to meet his eyes. She removed her hand from his. She remembered the reason for her fall now. She remembered the pain and shock she felt, hearing that news report on the radio. His presence here confused her. Why had he come back? None of it made sense.

"Rena? What is it?" His question was marked with concern.

She stared out the hospital window, looking at the new dawn breaking through. Birds chirped and tree branches swayed in the breeze. It was a glorious day to be alive, yet Rena's stomach knotted with heartbreaking anguish. "I was so hurt when you left. I guess I never got over you leaving me. And I thought it was happening all over again. I didn't know what to do with myself, so I started to paint the baby's room." She turned her head slightly to gaze into his eyes. Might as well give him the whole truth. "I figured I was on my own again. I wasn't meant to be with anyone. It would just be the baby and me from now on. I didn't want to rely on you or anyone else."

Tony clenched his teeth. Pain entered his eyes, but she continued. "The radio was on when I climbed the ladder, and I heard a news report about you. They said you were contemplating a racing comeback. When I heard that I felt faint. It was like my world was spinning in ten different directions. I couldn't get a grip. My worst fears had come true. That's when I fell."

Tony's eyes rounded. Shock stole over his face. He let go a vivid curse then took her chin in his hands and ever so gently lifted her face to his. "I'm so sorry, Rena. Sorry for everything. But you have to believe me. What you heard is not true. None of it is. My words were misconstrued. The press never gets anything right. That's why I had an argument with the newscaster. We almost came to blows, Rena. I called him every four-letter name in the book and then some.

"I swear to you that after the incident I took the next flight home. I didn't want you to hear that news report. It was a flat out falsity. But I didn't know if I could convince you how much I care about you from thousands of miles away."

"What about your obligations? You signed contracts."

He shrugged, his eyes hard. "Let them sue me. I can afford it. Losing a lawsuit is a million times better than losing you." He cast her a warm, sincere look. "I love you, Rena. I love you with all my heart."

He removed the sheet covering her and bent his head, laying the sweetest, most gentle kiss on her belly. "I love this baby, too. I love you both. I'll spend the rest of my life trying to convince you. But I'm asking for another chance. Give me a chance, sweetheart."

Tears entered her eyes. The loving gesture broke down all her defenses. Every wall she'd constructed against Tony fell to ruin, and her heart swelled. "Tony, is it true? Really true?"

"Yes, it's true. I love you. I want a life with you. A *real* life and not because of David's dying wish but because I have genuine love in my heart for you. I've always loved you, Rena."

He kissed her then, and it was the most tender brushing of their lips.

"I love you, too, Tony. I always have. Through everything, all the wrongs your family imposed on mine and all the hurt we've shared, I've never really stopped loving you. I think—" she began, admitting this truth to herself as well as to Tony "—I think David knew that. I think he knew that what we had couldn't be matched. And yet, I did love him. He was a good man."

"Yes, I know. He was the best. And I think he really wanted this for us. His child—*our* child—will have two parents who love each other as much as we love him or her."

Rena stroked Tony's dark hair, staring into his eyes, loving this strong powerful man with all that she had inside. "We can have a beautiful life."

"We will. I promise you. You and the baby will always come first."

"I believe you, Tony." She laughed as joy entered her heart. "I never thought I'd say that, but I really do believe in the strength of our love."

"And can you forgive me for everything in the past?"

Rena drew in a breath. "I think so. I think I already have."

"You won't be sorry, sweetheart. I will love and protect you the rest of my life. It's my solemn vow."

"Then I'm ready, Tony," she said decidedly.

"I am, too," he agreed, then shot her a puzzled look. "For *what*, exactly?"

"To shop for baby furniture. I want to fill our house with every baby thing imaginable."

Tony chuckled and drew her into his arms. "Now, I *know* you really love me."

"I do. I really, really do."

* * * * *

Kay Young returned to woozy consciousness to find that she was lying on a soft sofa beneath a heap of quilts near a cheerfully burning fire. When she tried to move, however, everything hurt, and she groaned.

At once she heard a sound, then a stranger with a hard, harsh face was squatting beside her. "Shh," he said softly. "You're safe here. I promise."

"I have to go," she said weakly, struggling against pain. "He'll find me. He can't find me."

"Easy, lady," he said quietly. "You're hurt. No one's going to find you here."

"He will," she said desperately, terror clutching at her insides. "He always finds me!"

"Easy," he said again. "There's a blizzard outside. No one's getting here tonight, not even the doctor. I know, because I tried."

"Doctor? I don't need a doctor! I've got to get away."

"There's nowhere to go tonight," he said levelly. "And if I thought you could stand, I'd take you to a window and show you."

But even as she tried once more to pull away the quilts, she remembered something else: this man had been gentle when he'd found her beside the road, even when she had kicked and clawed. He hadn't hurt her.

Terror receded just a bit. She looked at him and detected signs of true concern there.

The terror eased another notch and she let her head sag on the pillow. "He always finds me," she whispered.

"Not here. Not tonight. That much I can guarantee."

Will Kay's mysterious rescuer protect
her from her worst fears?
Find out in HER HERO IN HIDING
by New York Times *bestselling author Rachel Lee.*
Available June 2010, only from
Silhouette® Romantic Suspense.

Four friends, four dream weddings!

On a girly weekend in Las Vegas, best friends Alex, Molly,
Serena and Jayne are supposed to just have fun and forget
men, but they end up meeting their perfect matches!
Will the love they find in Vegas stay in Vegas?

Find out in this sassy, fun and wildly romantic miniseries
all about love and friendship!

Saving Cinderella! by MYRNA MACKENZIE
Available June

Vegas Pregnancy Surprise by SHIRLEY JUMP
Available July

Inconveniently Wed! by JACKIE BRAUN
Available August

Wedding Date with the Best Man
by MELISSA McCLONE
Available September

www.eHarlequin.com

HRI7663

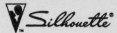

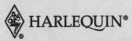

Love Inspired

Bestselling author

JILLIAN HART

brings you another heartwarming story
from

the
GRANGER
FAMILY
RANCH

Rancher Justin Granger hasn't seen his high school sweetheart
since she rode out of town with his heart. Now she's back, with
sadness in her eyes, seeking a job as his cook and housekeeper.
He agrees but is determined to avoid her...until he discovers
that her big dream has always been him!

The Rancher's Promise

*Available June
wherever books are sold.*